THE FAKER

BOSTON HAWKS HOCKEY

BOOK 3

GINA AZZI

The Faker

Copyright © 2021 by Gina Azzi

All rights reserved.

No part of this publication may be reproduced, distributed, or transmitted in any form or by any means, including photocopying, recording, or other electronic or mechanical methods, without the prior written permission of the publisher, except in the case of brief quotations embodied in critical reviews and certain other noncommercial uses permitted by copyright law.

This is a work of fiction. Names, characters, businesses, places, events, locales, and incidents are either the products of the author's imagination or used in a fictitious manner. Any resemblance to actual persons, living or dead, or actual events is purely coincidental.

ISBN: 978-1-954470-59-0

Alternate Cover

PROLOGUE

TORSTEN

"What are my options?" I ask my lawyer, a stand-up guy I've been working with since I first came to the United States. I was nineteen years old with dreams of being the next Bobby Orr. Bill Cantrell took me under his wing and kept an eye on me as I struggled in a new country, with no family, and too much money to carefully manage.

Bill blows out a sigh. I can tell he's weighing his words carefully and his hesitancy causes me to grip the phone tighter. "You really don't think you're going to re-sign, Torsten? The Hawks haven't given you any indication that they're cutting you loose, have they?"

I lean back against the couch cushion and squeeze my right knee. Twinges of pain spark and my kneecap pops when I straighten my leg. I let my hand fall back to my side. The tough conversation I had with Scott Reland, the Hawks owner; Coach Phillips; and senior management just this morning, flickers in my mind. I clear my throat. "I spoke to Reland. I'm not re-signing, Bill."

"What?" Surprise is heavy in Bill's tone. "When? What did Reland say?"

The gnawing ache that has taken up residence in my stomach since the start of this season swells upward into my chest. I had my doubts about my ability to keep playing hockey since September. Now that we're in April, I've had to swallow some difficult truths that I still haven't admitted to anyone save for the small group of people in Scott's office this morning. Now, Bill knows the truth too. "My knee is giving me issues again, Bill. Ever since I cracked my kneecap in that game against St. Louis, it hasn't been right."

"That was over three years ago."

"Exactly. I've had too many surgeries, too much scar tissue. My shoulder, my rotator cuff, is fucked. It's time..." I sigh. I never thought I'd see the day I'd hang up my skates. I guess none of us do but then suddenly, it's here and God, it *hurts*. "I'm finishing this season. Reland and Coach agreed to give me as much playing time as possible during the playoffs. Of course, I'm gunning for a Cup win. Afterwards, I'll break the news to the team. My contract isn't officially up until the end of June anyway."

"Jesus," Bill breathes out. "Damn. I'm sorry, kid. Why didn't you say anything sooner?"

I snort. "Wasn't ready to admit it." I tell him the truth. "I've spent the past seven months thinking through every goddamn scenario that would let me keep playing. But, after the last few games, the hits I've taken, the recovery that just isn't coming, I know it's time."

"You had one hell of a career, Torsten. You should be proud."

The corners of my mouth turn up at Bill's praise. In many ways, he's the closest male I have to a father figure since my father couldn't give a shit about my career in the NHL. Still, his words fan the ache in my chest until it's crawling up my throat and forming into a lump I have to swallow against. I *had* a hell of a career.

Except now that's nearly over, it doesn't seem like I have enough to show for it. I'm still alone in the United States with my entire family in Norway. I'm still single, no kids, no real legacy to leave behind. With the exception of a promise I made to my grandmother, my farmor, when I was eighteen, I don't even have any commitments.

"You really don't want to go back to Oslo?" Bill asks, cutting through my thoughts.

I think of Farmor. I think of Oslo and my childhood home. The last three visits I've made, Farmor was the only family member to see me, to speak to me. As much as I hate to consider a world without her in it, she's nearly ninety. After she passes, there will be *nothing* left for me in Norway, save for hurtful memories and broken promises. "Nope. I want to stay here. So, please, what are my legal options?"

"Are you looking into coaching? We can try to file for a green card through Employment-Based Immigration. Your best bet would be to prove your 'extraordinary ability' through hockey. But it's six to eight months processing time during which, you can't travel internationally."

I lean back in my chair and brush my fingers over my mouth.

"The last two times we went down this path..." Bill trails off.

"I had to get back to Norway."

"Yeah." Bill's quiet for a long moment. "Honestly, Torsten, your best plan is to wait it out. Commit to the process. Unless you're planning on getting married, there aren't many viable options."

Get married? I know Bill meant it as a joke but the words sting. My reputation as a well-versed flirt and perpetual bachelor do a spectacular job at concealing the truth. That I'd love to find the right woman, settle down, and build a home, a family, a future. Why else would someone date as much as I do, if not in search of a life partner?

Unfortunately for me, I still haven't found her. After the sting of Bill's words recede, I turn them over logically. In this case, marriage *is* a faster, more certain method to obtaining a green card than filing a bunch of paperwork that will most likely stall in the immigration process. Besides, I can't agree to *not* leave the United States for eight months and Bill knows it. Farmor's health has steadily declined over the past few years. Each time she calls, I jump on the first flight to Oslo. If she needs me, I'll be by her side, immigration be damned.

"Torst? That was a joke," Bill reminds me.

I force a chuckle. "Yeah, yeah I know. I was just thinking."

"About?"

"My grandmother."

"Ah. How is Greta doing?"

"Not that great," I admit. It pains me to think about her. To accept that I've built a life so far from her. The last visit I made to Oslo, I could hardly believe the physical changes in her appearance. She looked nothing like the motherly figure from my childhood. Her hair is entirely white now, her body frail. But her blue eyes still sparkle with mischief and I hold on to that.

"Still your biggest fan?" Bill asks.

I snicker. "She's still my only fan as far as the Hansens are concerned." It's not a secret that I'm not close with my family. Save for Farmor, I doubt they'd even remember I exist. Because the Hansens are practically nobility and I'm the black sheep who ran away to America and never looked back. Well, except for the handful of years I played hockey in Europe. It was at Farmor's urging, an attempt to make things right with my father, to reestablish the close bond I had with my brother Anders as children. Clearly, it didn't work and as soon as Farmor gave her blessing, I came back to the US.

"Do you want to start the paperwork?"

I sigh. This will be the third time I initiate this process. I wonder if my past two failures to stay put in the US will count against me. "What do you think?"

"I think you need to be sure. If we start this, you can't

back out again. It doesn't look good. Are you able to commit to staying in the US until it's sorted?"

I swear. "Let me think about it, okay?"

Bill's quiet for a second before he clears his throat. "Okay. For now, just focus on the playoffs. If this really is your last season..."

"Then we need to win the Cup," I agree with his unspoken words.

I hang up with Bill and stand from the couch in my swanky living room. I live in one of the penthouses in a luxury condo building on the Waterfront. Floor-to-ceiling windows wrap around the open concept of my kitchen and living room, offering spectacular views of downtown Boston and a bit of Boston Harbor.

Almost three years ago, when I turned thirty-five, I gained access to my trust fund. The one Farmor safeguarded as other members of my family tried to dismantle it. Every time I speak to her, she reminds me, "You're still a Hansen. You're just the best one."

Being a Hansen typically means having unbelievable wealth thrust upon you.

It's adhering to a strict set of expectations. It entails attending the most prestigious universities, being a member of the elitist social circles, and marrying into the right kind of family.

Unless you're me. Apparently, being the best Hansen means being on your own.

"You're seriously going to work *now*?" my best friend Claire asks.

I shove my bag into the passenger seat and cradle the phone between my face and shoulder as I flip on the ignition.

My old car, a POS I affectionately call Sally, sputters.

"Come on! Don't do this to me, Sal." I bang my palm on the top of the steering wheel.

"You still haven't gotten your car checked out?" Claire's voice is incredulous and I close my eyes.

Take a deep breath. Everything is fine.

I turn the ignition again, tears of relief springing to the corners of my eyes when ol' Sally revs up.

"Claire, I'm sorry. I'll make it up to you. It's just that—"

"Douchebag Stu called. Ri, why are you still working for this guy? He's been promising you a promotion for months and still, nada nada enchilada. You're running yourself ragged trying to meet all of his crazy deadlines and demands. It's Friday night! I've seen you once in the past two weeks."

Misery clamps down on my heart. Claire's right. For the past ten months, since I graduated college, I've busted my ass at Hendrix Marketing to prove that I'm worthy of my position. I'm in the office by 6 a.m. most mornings and always stay late.

Stu keeps telling me to hang in there just a little longer and the rewards will come. The promotion that he's been dangling under my nose for the past six months keeps me grinding even when the exhaustion settles in.

I don't need a reward in terms of recognition. I just need the fat paycheck for my student loans. But over the past few months, my patience has been waning and Stu's hands have become grabbier.

Last month, he rubbed the backs of his fingers over my ass and tried to pass it off as an accident. Twice. Three days ago, he referred to me as sexy.

He's repulsive but if I'm being honest, the person I'm most disappointed in is myself. I know I should quit. If I told Claire the truth about Stu, she would make me quit. But I *need* this job, in a way Claire doesn't understand. Mainly, because I've never told her. I am *drowning* in debt.

"Let me just run to the office really quick and see what he needs. I'll message you. There's still a good chance I can make it to Jolene's in time."

"Okay," Claire agrees, drawing out the word. "I really hope you can come, Ri. And that's not me trying to guilt you either. I just miss you. And Indy's not as much fun to drink with since a ginger ale is as wild as she gets."

I snort. "She's pregnant, Claire."

"I know, I know. But still…"

"I'm going to try to make it," I promise. "I'm going to the office right now." I pull my seat belt across my chest. "I'll message you as soon as I know what's going on."

"All right. You know, you can always accidentally drop a coffee on Stu's crotch…"

I laugh. "You have no idea how many times I've considered it."

"See you soon."

I disconnect the call and point my car in the direction of my office.

Stu Sanders has been running, and ruining, my life for nearly a year now. He better be summoning me for something good because my patience is on thin ice.

I'M NOT GOING *to drop this scalding hot coffee on Stu Sanders' crotch because that would be immature.*

He's my boss. I'm supposed to respect him. I'm supposed to learn from him.

Even though right now he's leering at me like a fucking perv.

Deep breath. I need this job. I need the money. I have bills. Loans.

Stu's eyes drink in my hips and linger on my breasts in the most unprofessional and repulsive manner.

I place down the mug near his elbow, which is casually resting on his desk. It makes a thud and a few droplets of coffee splatter his desk blotter.

The noise catches his attention and he lifts his beady eyes to mine.

My lips are pressed tightly together so I don't actually say the thoughts screaming in my head. "What do we need to go over that is so urgent?"

Stu licks his lips and lets his eyes linger on mine for a beat too long. "Why? You got plans tonight?"

"Yeah, Stu. I do and I'm already late." I shuffle back and cross my arms over my chest. I raise my eyebrows at him, waiting for him to get to the point where he explains why he summoned me here.

He clears his throat and tilts his head. "A date?"

I mash my lips together and don't respond.

"Have you ever been with an older, more mature man, Rielle? Someone who would know what to do with a woman like you in bed?"

I gasp. Is he fucking kidding me? My skin crawls when I note the hunger in his eyes, as if he's imagining me, right now, laid out beneath him. Vomit in my mouth. My flash of anger is quickly doused with a healthy dose of fear. I need to get the hell out of here.

I begin to turn away, when Stu's hand wraps around the back of my thigh. The moment his fleshy fingers hold my leg, I startle and stumble back, my heel catching on the carpet.

He lunges for me, his other arm wrapping around my waist to keep me from falling.

"No need to fall at my feet, honey." His breath, stale cigarettes, washes over my face. He's too close, practically panting, and panic rises in my chest.

I step backwards, trying to put space between us but he tightens his hold.

"Nowhere to go now, Rielle. We're the only ones here and I know you want this." His hand slides to my ass.

What the fuck? I lay both hands on his chest and push. "Get away from me, Stu. I'm not interested." My voice is clear but it wavers at the end, giving away just how nervous I am.

His hands clamp down in retaliation. "Don't be like this, Rielle. I know you need this job. Need *me*."

Fear snakes through my stomach as I struggle against his grip. He's holding my arms so tightly that his fingertips will leave bruises. "I don't fucking need you. Get your hands off me." I snarl, thrashing. My knee connects with his groin and he wheezes out, folding over.

I slip from his hold and back away slowly. I know I should run. I need to get the hell out of here. But... "Stu, this isn't going—"

"You're fired, Rielle," Stu bellows, righting himself. "For

ten fucking months, you teased me with those sexy skirts and high heels. And now, you don't want to play?" He shakes his head. "I'm not paying for this shit when I can have an assistant who's *willing* to do the work I need."

My mouth drops open. I'm more shocked than I've ever been before. Even more so than the night my father informed me I would major in pre-med or he was cutting me off financially. "Are you kidding me right now?" My anger flares and it feels good to release it. To let my resentment toward Stu seep out instead of keeping it bottled at the back of my throat, like a gag. "I'm not your assistant, Stu. I'm a marketing associate."

He waves a hand dismissively, his eyes narrowed into slits.

"And I don't need to put up with this shit." I throw my hand out at him, feeling bolder now that the office space is between us. "I wouldn't fuck you if you were the last man on Earth and Homo sapiens were going extinct." I turn sharply on my heel and stride from his office.

The moment I clear the threshold, it dawns on me that we may be the only two people in the entire building. My hands begin to tremble and my anger recedes as fear skates down my spine. I swipe my coat and purse from my desk and book it to the elevators, jabbing at the down arrow.

It isn't until I'm in my car with the doors locked, that reality sinks in. Oh, God. Bile crawls up my throat and my hands shake. I feel jittery, off-balanced, and nauseous. What am I going to do? I need this job. I need the money.

My second—or maybe third?—eviction notice, a flimsy pink slip of paper I ripped off my apartment door and clenched in my fist just six weeks ago when hockey heartthrob Torsten Hansen escorted me home blinks in my mind. I was drunk. And rambling. I was starting to crack.

But now, I'm shattered. Because there was another slip on

my door this morning. This time, I left it. I'm going to default on my loan payment. I'm going to miss rent again.

I'm going to be evicted, with nowhere to live but an alleyway.

Tears collect in my eyes. The urge to cry, to sob and wail and hit something, rises in my throat but at the last second, I swallow it down. I may have left the Carter household but at my core, I'm still a Carter. And Carters keep things close to the chest. We figure out our own problems and never air anything in public. Not our thoughts, not our feelings, and most certainly not our shortcomings.

Deep breath. I'll be okay. I'll sort this out.

The shrill ringing of my cell causes me to jump and I answer it. "Claire."

"Ri-Ri! I'm so sorry to be the one to bail but Indy's got heartburn and East just got home from an AA meeting and seems overwhelmed so—"

A trickle of relief rolls through me. The last thing I want to do is sit in a noisy bar and shout to Claire and Indy that I was fired, assaulted, and will soon be homeless. God, I wish I could tell them the truth. About my family, my finances, my lack of options. But if I did, they'd help me, no questions asked. I'd ruin the only true friendships I have by altering the dynamic beyond repair. I've witnessed firsthand how money ruins families, friendships, and it's not something I'm willing to risk with Claire or Indy. I clear my throat. "No worries, babe. Honestly, I'm exhausted anyway."

"Well, I'll still make it up to you."

"We'll reschedule soon." I don't mention that my calendar is now wide open. "Go be with your man."

Claire giggles and I can't help the pang that hits me in the chest. Of course I'm happy for her and Easton. They've worked hard at their relationship and have overcome a lot of obstacles. I understand that Claire needs to be there for him. I *want* her to be there for East.

But sometimes, in moments like this, when I realize how soul-crushingly alone I am, I wish that she would notice I'm starting to drown. I wish *someone* would realize that I'm about to be pulled under entirely.

"Call you tomorrow, Ri."

"Good night, Claire." I disconnect and take a shaky breath. Then, I ease out of the parking lot.

Part of me is desperate to go home, shower, and crawl into bed. The other part of me hates the thought of being on my own right now, with all the silence, all the mistakes, closing in on me.

I drive past the turn to my apartment. What the hell am I doing? I can't just drive aimlessly and waste Sally's gas. I stop at a red light and grip the steering wheel. I bang my head back against the headrest. Tears pool in the corners of my eyes. What am I going to do? Jerry Jensen is expecting a loan payment on Monday and I'm still over $200 short.

I could always sell Sally. My stomach twists at the thought. But then what? It will only buy me a few months. I need a *plan*. For the first time in my life, I come up blank.

You want to study marketing? Dad's laughter rings in my head. *What useless life are you going to have with that? You'll make no money.* The contempt in his gaze was obvious.

But I was rebellious. So certain that I could carve my own path and blaze my own trail. I was taking my future in my hands and doing it my way. My choice of university, my choice of degree, my choice of who I lived with.

A sob escapes my throat as I recall those four magical years. Living with Claire. Feeling inspired and passionate about my courses. Interning in Paris. Dabbling in photography. It was like another life.

The one that came before reality crashed around me and I realized I owed nearly half a million dollars to one of my childhood friend's families for bankrolling my educational pursuits against my father's wishes.

Was Dad right?

The thought cuts deep because if so, I've made a hell of a lot more mistakes than just staying in a thankless position under Stu Sanders for ten months.

The sign for Taps, a neighborhood pub that has gained notoriety over the years since the Boston Hawks Hockey team usually grab drinks here, flickers in the distance. I've spent a lot of time at this pub with Claire since her brother Austin is the team captain and Easton is the left wing.

Sighing, I pull into the parking lot. Clearly, I shouldn't spend any money on a glass of wine. And I shouldn't stay out this late because my apartment is in a less than desirable area and the last thing I need is to fight off a second man with grabby hands tonight.

But the feel of Stu's hands still ripples over my skin. I shiver, knowing I'll go crazy if I'm alone right now.

I step out of the car, tie the sash on my coat, shoulder my bag, and scurry into Taps. The atmosphere is warm. The bartender, Pete, is a familiar face. And no one looks at me, a girl with tears in her eyes, twice.

I take a seat at the end of the bar and shrug out of my coat. Exhaling slowly, I tuck my hair behind my ears and wave to Pete. As soon as I have a glass of merlot in hand, my body relaxes slightly. I take a deep sip and let the bold taste roll down my throat.

I'm going to be okay. I'll figure something out.

But what?

Not for the first time, I wish Mom were still alive. Although, if she were, there's no way things would have fallen apart between Dad and me. Not like this, anyway. I close my eyes for a beat and envision her calm voice, the feel of her fingers running through my hair. Every time I ran to her, angry over some argument I had with Dad, she would laugh that we were too similar, both of us hardheaded and passionate. But I never agreed. I wanted to be my mother's daughter through and through, even after she was taken from me when I was fourteen.

I bite the corner of my mouth and force my eyes open. I take another sip of my wine.

The adrenaline that's been buzzing through my limbs since Stu touched me begins to recede. Exhaustion sweeps through me. The door to Taps opens and a few of the guys sitting near me whisper excitedly. When I turn my head, I realize why.

Torsten Hansen, a defenseman for the Hawks and sex on a stick, just walked in.

Jesus. My cheeks flame. Could this night get any worse?

Six weeks ago, I went out and got stupidly drunk with Claire. When Claire bounced early, I stayed behind, drinking my body weight in tequila and vodka shots. Torsten Hansen, chivalrous guy that he is, made sure I got home okay.

He didn't even make a face when he flipped on the lights to my small apartment. I'm the girl who lives in Southie. He's the guy who owns the apartment buildings a handful of streets over on the Waterfront. In that moment, the disparity between us, between me and my own family, was glaringly obvious. And it *hurt*. It scraped at my soul to know that my own pride was responsible for my current living conditions. For my lack of options.

And Torsten Hansen, with his broad shoulders and ridiculous six-pack, witnessed it firsthand. I dip my head and take another gulp of wine. I've got to get out of here. I need to go home, throw myself in the shower, sleep for a million years, and regroup.

But when I look back up, my eyes slam into two pools of icy blue. Surprise ripples across Torsten's expression as recognition flares in his eyes. At the kindness in his face, a wave of emotion swells in my throat. Tears prick the corners of my eyes, threatening to fall. God, what is wrong with me?

I try to shake it off but I can't. I feel unbalanced, like

gravity is giving up on me along with the rest of the universe. Old inadequacies and insecurities wrap around me. My failures are on full display for anyone to pick apart.

It must show in my expression because Torsten's mouth twists and he moves to slide off his barstool.

Oh, no. I shake my head and gesture I'll come to him. There's an empty seat beside him and even though he's definitely not someone I'd want to see me unravel, at least he's not Claire.

I take a deep breath, pick up my wine glass and coat, and hope I don't make myself look like even more of a fool.

Although, at this point, is that even possible?

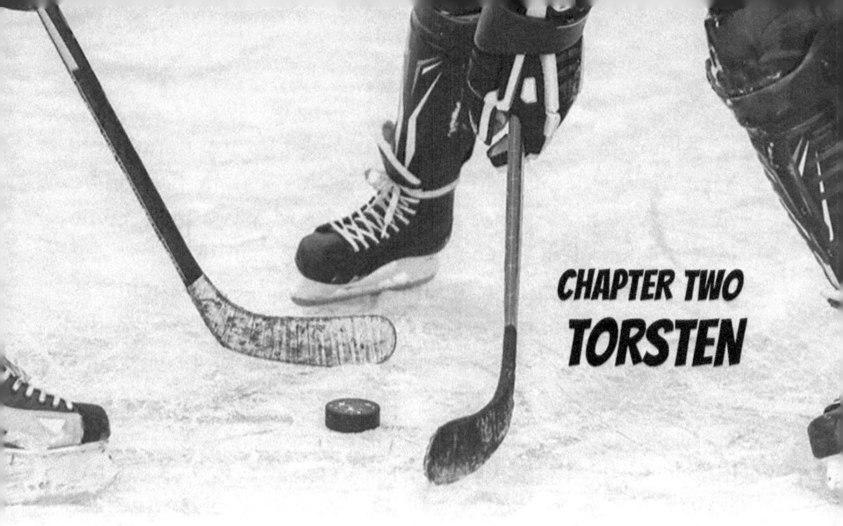

CHAPTER TWO
TORSTEN

T he beer is cold and tangy. It goes down smooth, just the way I like it.

I grin at Pete, the bartender, and gesture that I'm ready for a shot. Last night, my hockey team, the Boston Hawks, won our first playoff game. Afterwards, we celebrated with a few beers, but tonight, everyone is with their families.

Everyone except me. My family, if you can call them that, are all in Norway and at nearly thirty-eight years old, I still haven't found the right woman to settle down with here in America.

I snort at myself. The right woman doesn't exist. At least for me she doesn't. I've been burned too many times to place my future happiness in one woman's hands. I'm more of a happily-for-now than a happily-ever-after kind of guy and I've made peace with that.

"Thanks, Pete." The bartender places down a shot glass, the necessary saltshaker, and a lime wedge.

"You got it, Hansen. Congrats on the playoffs."

I dip my head in thanks and shift my weight, groaning at the soreness that ripples through my body. I guess that's the silver lining of this being my last season; soon, I won't be in physical pain all the time.

Although, a new slew of issues occupies my mind these days. How will I stay in the US after this season? Last night, right before my game, Farmor called and asked if I'll come visit this summer. Her voice was quieter than usual, as if it took too much energy to fill it with the laughter and lightness I'm used to. I pinch the bridge of my nose and shake the thought away. Right now, I need to focus on the playoffs, on the Cup.

I raise the shot of tequila to my mouth and freeze, all my troubles flying right out of my mind. Because Rielle Carter is at the other end of the bar, looking like every fantasy I've had of her come to life. She must feel my stare because she looks up and her dark eyes, nearly black, pierce mine. Even with the space and people between us, I can tell something's wrong.

Six weeks ago, I escorted her drunk ass home when she had too much to drink with her best friend and my captain's little sister, Claire. But from years of casual encounters, I know that Rielle projects confidence. She's a charming and carefree woman who gets under your skin the moment you meet her.

Tonight, she's none of those things. Her shoulders curve inward and her arm wraps protectively around her torso, as if she wants to disappear into herself. For a woman who always stands tall and proud, I'm startled by this version of her. Tonight, she looks heartbreakingly sad. She offers me a small smile that doesn't reach her eyes.

My concern spikes and I lean forward, staring intently at her watery eyes, her puffy lips. *Has she been crying?*

The thought causes me to slide from my barstool but she shakes her head and indicates that she'll come to me. I turn toward Pete and order more shots.

I watch Rielle as she moves closer, a coat thrown over her arm, a wine glass in hand. I take in the curves of her hips, sheathed in a sexy pencil skirt that ends just below her knees.

She's rocking a silk blouse that clings to her curves. Nude heels click against the beat-up wooden floor as she draws nearer. Black hair, black eyes, and a luscious mouth I've thought more than once about tasting, Rielle Carter is a bombshell.

But right now, she looks miserable and my worry for her overshadows my wayward thoughts.

"Hey Big Daddy," she greets me, dropping the lame nickname started by Claire. Of course, it stuck and now the whole team uses it.

"What're you drinking, Ri?" I ask, pulling the barstool next to mine closer.

She shrugs, placing down her wine glass. She hangs her coat on the back of the barstool and slips onto the seat. "Just a merlot."

"What's wrong?" I gentle my tone.

She stares at me. Her eyes are empty, her expression aloof. Pete delivers more shots and Rielle snorts. She picks one up, running the pad of her index finger around the rim. She shrugs, offering me a lopsided grin. "What's right?"

I frown at her answer and watch as she throws back the shot and picks up another one. She downs it quickly, not bothering with the salt or the lime. Then she turns on her barstool, her knee brushing against my leg.

"Congrats on the playoffs."

"Thanks."

"Are you by yourself tonight?" she asks, looking around for my teammates. We frequent Taps a lot and since I hate being alone, I usually recruit some of the guys to come with me.

I nod.

"Me too."

I lean back in my seat and study her. Her eyes swim with emotion. She looks lost and lonely. *Pained.* My mind travels back to six weeks ago. Rielle was tipsy as hell. And adorable.

She was happy, her big eyes shining, as she danced in the middle of a crowded dance floor, unconcerned by all the men circling her, desperate for a morsel of her attention. She closed her eyes, waved her arms overhead, and rotated her hips until I couldn't tear my gaze away. I remember how she dissolved into laughter when she caught my eye. She danced her way over to me, beckoning for me to join her. And at the envious glares of the other nearby men, I did so gladly. Her laughter from that night still interrupts my dreams, causing a strange sense of longing when I wake in the morning.

But when I escorted her home, I witnessed a version of her I never considered. The larger-than-life, dazzling woman is living paycheck to paycheck. Just scraping by. Her small apartment in Southie tells a completely different story than the woman who always shows up with her head held high, rocking designer threads and an untouchable veneer.

Tonight, I'm catching a glimpse of *that* woman. The woman who is struggling and doing her best to keep it all together. I know this because for too damn long, I was her. The hockey player with the trust fund who "has it all," but doesn't have a damn thing that matters. No family, no relationship, no one to kiss hello when I walk in the door from a grueling practice or a brutal away game. Although the circumstances are different, I know what it feels like to be invisible in a crowd. Right now, Rielle is wearing *that* look. Dejection and hurt, sorrow and loneliness.

She shifts to reach for her wine glass and I narrow my eyes. Are those bruises on her arm? My heightening concern is swept away by a rush of anger. Who the fuck dared to put his hands on her?

"Who the fuck marked your arm?" I growl.

She gasps, tugging on the sleeve of her shirt. Her eyes widen and her mouth opens and closes. Her body stiffens and she eyes the door over my shoulder, looking like she wants to bolt.

Shit. I can't let her rush out of here, not when she's hurting. I swear and grip the armrest of her barstool. "Whatever you're thinking, don't."

"Don't what?" she whispers.

"Don't leave. Not on your own, not like this. Hang with me for a bit? Take another shot."

She narrows her gaze and considers me. I stare straight back, trying to tell her with my eyes all the things I'm sure as fuck not going to say. *I'm worried about you. I want to beat the shit out of the dick who put his hands on you. There's no way in hell I'm letting you go home alone right now.*

Finally, she nods and settles back in her seat. I place another shot glass in front of her and line two up in front of me.

She snorts and picks up her shot glass. She raises it in my direction, the black in her eyes swallowing the flecks of golden brown. "To Daddy issues."

As much as I want her to confide in me about whatever the hell went down tonight, I dislike the blasé snark she's protecting herself in. I narrow my eyes at her and consider handing out a truth for a truth. "I can drink to that, Ri." I tap my glass against hers and toss it back.

Her eyes widen in surprise but she quickly hides it by taking the shot.

"Rielle, what happened tonight?"

She glances at the ceiling, as if holding back tears. "I lost my job."

I search my mind for everything I know about Rielle and the thing that I hold on to, the thing that Claire and her cousin Indy have said countless times is that she's a workaholic. Why the hell would she lose her job? "Why? What happened?"

She shakes her head and her eyes well with fresh tears. Pure horror washes over her features.

"Ri." I reach out and cup her cheek. "It's okay to be upset. You know that right?"

She nods and clears her throat, blinking furiously. "Logically, yes. I know that. But I don't, I'm not sure how…"

I swipe my thumb over her cheekbone. Her skin is soft and smooth and perfect. I drop my hand. "Tell me what you need. Right now, don't even think about it."

"Why are you being so nice to me?" she whispers.

I frown. "You must know I am the nicest guy on the Hawks."

She snorts. "That'd be Noah. Or Austin."

"Screw them," I joke and she gives me an almost-smile. I chew the corner of my mouth, giving her another truth. One I rarely share. "Because I know what it's like to be alone and hurting even when you're surrounded by people."

She draws in an inhale, understanding flaring in her irises. "I want to drink tequila until my head spins. And I want to sleep in late just one day, just tomorrow."

"Okay," I agree. I pick up my next shot glass just as Pete delivers a new batch. "To sleeping in."

She rolls her eyes but her expression clears the tiniest bit. She picks up another shooter and clinks it against mine.

We down them and I've got to give her credit, she doesn't flinch. After four shots in quick succession, she doesn't even look tipsy. But I know they'll kick in soon, soften some of the spiky edges that are jabbing at her.

"I'll make sure you get home okay," I tell her.

"This is becoming a habit," she says, opting for her wine glass.

"I don't mind it." I lean back in my seat. Even though I shouldn't be drinking heavily right at the start of the playoffs, there's no way I'm leaving Rielle to drink on her own. Not tonight, not when she needs someone to step up and be there for her. When Pete passes, I order another beer and tell him to keep the shots coming.

"I'm sure you have better things to do."

"Can't think of one at the moment," I reassure her. "So..." I drop my eyes to her arm again. As long as Rielle is beside me, I can remain calm. But there's no way in hell I'm leaving her on her own without knowing the story behind the asshole who bruised her.

"So..." Worry washes over her face. She doesn't want to talk and she most certainly doesn't want to overshare. She doesn't want to tell me *things*. Damn, *I get it*, I want to tell her. *I get you.*

Instead, I decide to confide in her about my predicament. "Let me get your opinion on something. If you had a friend, let's call him Stan—"

"Stan?" she asks skeptically.

"Stan's a nice name."

She snorts. "Keep going."

"Say Stan was in a bit of a pickle."

"Where did you learn English?"

I laugh. "I excel at idiomatic expressions."

She grins and relaxes a little. "Why is Stan in a pickle?"

I scrub my hand over my jawline. "Stan is caught between something he wants, something for his future, and his family and their expectations."

Her expression slips and her eyes narrow. I pause for a second, thrown by her intensity. I clear my throat.

"Anyway, Stan needs to make an important decision. It's one that will affect his career, his legacy so to speak. If he does it, it may hurt the only person in his family he truly cares about."

"And he doesn't know if he can live with that," she says, the softest slur wrapping around her words. Understanding dawns in her expression and she purses her lips thoughtfully. Her mouth is like a rosebud and I wonder what her lips would taste like.

I take a sip of my beer instead. "What do you think he should do?"

"What are his options? His career and livelihood or his word and his heart?"

I nod, drawn to her. Her expression, filled with understanding and compassion, soothes me. She gets it. Without even knowing the whole story, my truth, she understands the anguish I'm battling. A calmness fills me and I lean back in my seat. "And, there's one other option but it's a little bit shady."

She narrows her eyes. "How shady?"

"It would allow Stan to do both things, safeguard his future and fulfill a promise to his family member."

"But?"

"He would have to enter into a deal, an arrangement, that's complicated."

"Complicated," she murmurs. She tips her wine glass back and her eyes, dark and deep and burning, find mine over the rim.

"Illegal," I amend.

She drains the glass and sets it back on the bar. "I see."

"Do you?" I ask, hoping more than I should for her to really *see*.

She nods slowly.

"What should Stan do?" I press her for a response. I need an answer. One that comes from someone who isn't me.

"Stan should do whatever it takes to survive. To physically make it but also to preserve his integrity. His word. He shouldn't sacrifice everything he's done nor should he compromise his name by reneging on a promise."

"So"—I lick my lips, my ears suddenly ringing—"Stan may need to bend some rules?"

She picks up a shot glass. "I would."

I grin, adoring her in this moment. "Me too."

She throws back the tequila and wipes the back of her

hand over her mouth. I don't want to tell her to slow down but I also know she's going to feel like shit in the morning. I gesture to Pete that we're good for a bit.

"I'm starting to feel these," Rielle says.

"I would imagine so."

The corner of her mouth lifts. "And because I am, I'm going to tell you the truth. The reason I'm so torn up about my job isn't just because of the job. I need this paycheck."

Hope swells in my chest that she's confiding in me, but I know I have to play it cool or she'll clam back up. I force myself not to look at the bruises on her arm. "I get it. You have bills."

She scoffs. "I have more than bills."

"This is just a bump in the road, Ri. You're going to find another job. In the meantime, I don't want to make you feel uncomfortable, but I can help you out until you get back on your feet." Hell, I can move her into one of my units if her rent is causing her so much stress.

At the offer, her eyes shutter closed and the honesty in them disappears completely. Her back snaps straight and she dips her head. Shit, I pushed too hard. Rielle doesn't want anyone's help. For whatever reason, she needs to know she can sort this out on her own.

I swear softly, my mind scrambling. *Don't double down, Hansen. Find your chill.* "Think about it, don't think about it. Just know, if you ever really need a safety net, you have one," I tell her. "Now, let's drink and sing karaoke and forget all about Stan's bullshit and bills."

She glances up, a hesitant hope in her expression. "Sing karaoke?"

I grin, scraping a hand along my jaw. "I'll battle you."

She throws her head back and laughs. It's the most genuine and uninhibited she's been all night and a swell of pride ripples in my chest that I caused it. I made her laugh. "Battle me? Torsten, I can carry a tune."

"So can I," I challenge her. "Hey Pete," I call out. "How do you feel about a little performance?"

Pete laughs and shrugs, tossing me the phone connected to the speakers. "Have at it, Torst. Just don't be upset when you go viral on social media tomorrow."

I grin. I'm definitely feeling the alcohol swimming in my veins. I chance a glance at Rielle. She's a bit tipsy but hanging in there. Girl can hold her liquor. I hand her the phone. "Pick your playlist."

She smiles and it makes my chest feel funny. Too tight.

Of course I shouldn't be drinking and singing in a pub. Not when the Hawks are in the playoffs and we have a game the day after tomorrow. But I've put hockey first for the last two decades of my life. Right now, I've got a gorgeous girl who's barely keeping her chin up, sitting in the chair next to me and battling demons.

I'll deal with the team's ire if it means making Rielle laugh. If it means learning who the hell hurt her tonight.

CLAIRE

Um, hi. Remember me? Your best friend? I feel like I don't know you because the last time I saw Rielle Carter sing karaoke, she was in a wet T-shirt contest in Cancun on spring break. And we were freshman. WHO ARE YOU? Btw, you look hella hot in that pencil skirt. It's very Librarian-esque. Indy may try to steal it.

I groan as the sunlight assaults my eyes. What the hell is Claire talking about?

I try to roll over in my bed but the movement hurts. Everything hurts. My head aches and my mouth is so dry I don't want to swallow. When I do, my throat burns. And my skin feels like it's been peeled back a few layers. I force myself to hit play on the video she sent and nearly fall out of bed when I see myself onscreen, shaking my ass and belting out the lyrics to Whitney Houston's "I Wanna Dance With Somebody."

What. The. Fuck?

I cringe but then Torsten enters the frame. He steps right onto the bar, amidst wild cheering and whistling from the handfuls of patrons at Taps. He sings backup to my perfor-mance and breaks it down with some dance moves that belong in the nineties.

I laugh despite the pang it causes in my temples.

Torsten and I are wasted. But we're having fun, real fun. The uninhibited, genuine, carefree kind of fun I haven't experienced since I tossed my college graduation cap in the air.

"Oh, good. You're alive."

I gasp and clutch my duvet to my chest. My eyes swing to the door where Torsten shadows the frame, looking way sexier than a man with a wicked hangover ought to.

"You're here?"

He shakes his head. "Did you think I'd drop you off and bolt? You drank *my* body weight in tequila."

I close my eyes and snippets of last night float through my mind.

Torsten ordering round after round of shots.

My skin crawling after what went down with Stu.

Losing my damn job.

Feeling lost and lonely.

Torsten cheering me up.

Stan. Who the hell is Stan?

Too many shots.

Dancing on the bar.

Cracking up. Inventing dance moves. Feeling like myself again.

I force my eyes open, even though it's still too bright in here, and glance at Torsten.

He hasn't moved from where he's holding up the wall. His arms are crossed over his chest. His black button-down is wrinkled and a sexy scruff coats his cheeks and chin. His hair is a mess, flattened on one side and sticking up in wild spikes on the other. His eyes are concerned, his mouth is twisted in amusement, and he looks like he doesn't know whether to turn on his heel and leave or crawl into bed next to me.

But he's here.

"Thank you," I say, pulling myself up to a seated position. "For last night. That was…you are the nicest Hawk."

He chuckles and steps into my room.

My duvet pools around my hips and when I look down, I see I'm wearing a T-shirt. I look back up at Torsten. "Did anything—"

"No," he cuts me off, horror washing over his face.

Well, it's a good thing I'm already feeling so down in the dumps because if not, his reaction to the idea of hooking up with me would have obliterated my ego.

"You needed something clean to wear after you threw up," he explains.

I wince. That explains the soreness in my throat. *Shit, how wasted was I last night?* Embarrassment floods through me, causing my cheeks to burn. I grip the duvet and force myself to meet Torsten's curious gaze. "You're a class act, Torsten. You shouldn't have had to deal with me last night. Thank you for looking out and for making sure I got home okay. Thank you for sleeping on my couch which must have been the most uncomfortable night's sleep of your life since it's only a loveseat."

He snorts. "I've slept on worse."

I wrinkle my nose and shake my head, the magnitude of last night and just how much I let my guard down steam-rolling me. "I'm really embarrassed. I swear, I don't usually make a spectacle of myself like that."

"Maybe you should do it more often," he challenges.

I narrow my eyes at him. "What? You're plastered all over social media singing back up to my Whitney. Claire sent me a video." I gesture to my phone.

He smiles. "Did you see how hard we were laughing?"

I nod, unable to stop myself from smiling back.

"Maybe we both needed that last night. The goofiness and the forgetting."

I swipe my tongue over my chapped lips. "Maybe."

Torsten walks closer and takes a seat at the foot of my bed. He shifts his weight so he's facing me. His expression is neutral but his eyes burn, curious and worried and devoid of judgement. "We need to talk, Ri."

I frown and feign ignorance. "About what?"

He pulls a slip of paper from his pocket and shows it to me.

I wince. The stupid eviction notice I never pulled off my door yesterday.

"This is the same type of notice as six weeks ago, isn't it? The one you ripped off the door and said was a delivery?"

I work a swallow and nod slowly, my embarrassment hiking up to new levels of pure mortification.

"You got another one?"

I clear my throat and nod again, unable to meet his eyes.

"Hey." He dips his head to catch my gaze. When I don't move, he reaches out and hooks his finger under my chin, forcing me to look at him.

He's calm and sincere. So damn thoughtful and genuine. His kindness makes my chest hurt and the feelings I've been burying for months begin to work their way to the surface. Over the past few months, Claire's been wrapped up in Easton and his recovery. Indy's been preoccupied with her pregnancy. Of course, I don't blame my friends for focusing on the big changes in their own lives.

But how is Torsten recognizing all the pieces I've tried to hide? How is he, an acquaintance at best, more attuned to my personal struggles than my closest friends? The realization makes me shift uncomfortably. Am I slipping up that badly? Cracking deeply enough that anyone paying a little attention can see the ugliness? Or is it more than that? Is it Torsten?

"Talk to me, Rielle. Please. I know we don't know each other that well but I swear to you, we're more similar than you think. So tell me what's going on because this"—he runs his fingertips over the bruises Stu made on my arm—"isn't going to fucking happen again."

I close my eyes, suddenly more overwhelmed than I was last night, rushing out of Stu's office. "Torsten," I say but my stomach interrupts the moment by grumbling loudly.

He drops his hand. "Come on. Let's go get breakfast. You need a gallon of water, a carafe of coffee, greasy food, and carbs. I know a place not far from here that has killer pancakes. Then, we'll talk. For real." He fixes me with a hard look until I nod.

"For real," I agree, swinging my legs to the side of my bed. The room spins and I take a moment for my vision to catch up to my movement. I groan as I force myself to stand.

Torsten snorts, grasping the underside of my arm and helping me to my feet. "I'm going to use your bathroom real quick. Take your time, Ri. We're both battling brutal hang-overs this morning."

I shoot him a grateful look and try to pull myself together.

SINCE WE'RE CARLESS, having taken an Uber to my place the night before, we walk to the restaurant. The cold air that whips around me wakes me up and helps ease the clanging in my head.

Torsten points to a little diner on the corner. "I know it doesn't look like much but the pancakes are phenomenal."

When he holds the door open for me, I slip inside the warm, cozy neighborhood diner.

"Nice game, Torsten." The woman behind the counter waves.

"Thanks, Beth. Is here okay?" He points to a booth in the back.

"Wherever you want, hon. I'll be right over with coffee."

"Thanks." Torsten hits her with his blinding smile and I swear, she swoons a little. Even though Beth looks old enough to be Torsten's grandmother, I can tell she's a little smitten with him.

Aren't we all?

I slide into the booth across from him. Beth comes over moments later with mugs of hot coffee. Torsten and I order pancakes.

He leans back in his seat and studies me.

"What?" I ask, reaching my hand to my face. Do I have something in my teeth?

"What happened to you, Ri? No bullshit. I'm looking at you and while you're as gorgeous as ever, I don't really recognize the woman I'm staring at."

Wow. No lead up there. "Are you always this blunt?"

"Call it like I see it."

"You know we don't really know each other that well, right?"

"I know it may seem that way. But, sweetheart, I know you a hell of a lot better than you think."

I lean forward, the table cutting into my chest. Torsten's eyes dip down to my cleavage before snapping back up to my eyes. "How do you figure that?"

He swallows and his thick fingers wrap around the handle of the coffee mug. "Because like recognizes like. I've been in a version of your shoes before." He shakes his head, giving me a look I don't understand. "Don't forget I'm an old man compared to you."

I roll my eyes. "You're not that old."

"Almost thirty-eight," he says it like he needs to remind me.

I shrug. I've dated two of my college professors who were well into their forties. Older guys don't scare me off. "So, what do you think you know?"

"I know that you're struggling, Ri. Financially, emotionally—you're hurting."

I take a gulp of my coffee, wincing when the hot brew burns my tongue.

"You're going to find another job, Ri. But if you're ripping eviction notices off your door two months in a row, that tells me you're behind the eight ball."

I bite my bottom lip as a line from our conversation last night floats through my mind. *Idiomatic expressions.*

"So, tell me about your bills. I know you don't want help. I know you are a proud, fierce woman. And I admire it, Rielle. You're independence is sexy as hell. But no one gets anywhere without a little help now and then. And it seems like you're not reaching out for support in any aspect of your life. So now, I'm going to force you to take it. I'm not going anywhere, sweetheart. Start talking." He takes a swig of his coffee.

And I choke on mine because what. the. hell? Who does he think he is just ordering me to spill my guts? And why is my heart beating faster at the concern in his eyes? At the fact that he noticed and *cares.*

Torsten leans closer and presses a napkin into my hand as I continue to sputter. Beth drops off two water glasses and I chug mine. After a few moments, I get my breathing under control.

Then, I glare at Torsten. Partially in horror. Mostly in embarrassment. And maybe, just a teeny tiny bit, in gratitude. I consider lying but at the scowl on his face, I know he'll see right through me. Clearly, hiding my secret isn't doing me any good and there's no dynamic to ruin with Torsten. It's not like I can ruin a casual acquaintance with someone. So I clear my throat and challenge him. "Yeah? You've got an extra $470,000 lying around?"

This time, it's his turn to choke. I grin bitterly and push over the napkin dispenser. Beth shoots us a confused look before shaking her head and dropping off two plates stacked with blueberry pancakes.

"Four hundred and seventy thousand dollars?" he hisses. "Who the hell do you owe that much money to?"

I smirk at him, feeling some of my sadness give way to a hardness I grasp onto with both hands. Moving from shaky ground to a higher elevation, I find my footing once more. I take a sip of my coffee, pour some maple syrup over my pancakes, and cut into them. "That's a long story."

He glances around the diner. "I've got time, Ri."

"Eat your pancakes, Torsten."

"No fucking way are we leaving it at this. Last night, you were almost sobbing at Taps because you lost your job. Some asshole clearly manhandled you." He glares at my arm. "I tugged a goddamn eviction notice off your door. Now, I find out you are hundreds of thousands of dollars in debt and you want me to just drop it?" His voice is colder than I've ever heard it.

I glance up, gasping at the ice in his eyes. Fury fills the lines of his face. His hand is clenched around his fork. "Torsten."

He shakes his head. "Not a chance in hell, Ri. Tell me what's going on." He leans closer, beseeching me with his eyes.

I wince, cursing myself for being honest. Once again, my stupid pride sets me back. Instead of being truthful, I dig deep for my bitchy abrasiveness. Anything to get him to stop caring, to change the subject, to walk out of here and never turn his pitying eyes my way again. "What's it matter to you, huh? I'm nobody to you. Just your captain's little sister's friend. A girl you sang karaoke with drunk at a bar."

His lips press into a firm line and his fork clatters to the table.

"You okay, Torsten? The pancakes all right?" Beth calls out.

Torsten glares at me, his expression furious. Slowly he releases an exhale and rolls his neck toward Beth. "Yes, Beth. The pancakes are great. Thank you."

"All right, hon. I'm just going on break before the lunch rush hits. Holler if you need me." Beth pushes through the double swinging doors toward the kitchen.

Torsten turns back toward me and my breath lodges in my throat. Outside of a hockey game, I've never seen him look so angry, so *intense*. His flashing eyes cause a thrill to shoot down my spine, a throb to clench in my lower abdomen. I press my thighs together and scrape my teeth over my bottom lip. Torsten zeroes in on the movement, his restraint slipping, his eyes swirling, dark blue like a violent ocean storm.

"Rielle Carter," he whispers and I like the way my name sounds on his lips. Like it so much more than I should. "If you think I don't care about you at all, then I've done a piss poor job at being your friend."

"Friend," I repeat, working a swallow.

Torsten grins but it's sinister. I've never seen this side of him before and I like it. "Sweetheart, come on now, I've always sought you out. At every Hawks event you show up to, I find you."

"You flirt with everyone," I remind him.

A growl escapes from his chest and his eyes narrow. Ooh, I've pissed him off. My thighs clench tighter and I wring my hands together. What the hell is wrong with me? How did this conversation go sideways so quickly? Minutes ago, I wanted to die of embarrassment, now I don't care if Torsten knows all about my mistakes if he just eases the inferno building in my bloodstream.

"You're right," he agrees and I feel like a tidal wave of cold water puts out the fire in my body.

His eyes clear some and he straightens his posture. I let out a shaky exhale, feeling unsteady. I reach for my water glass and fumble it. Torsten's hand darts out to grasp the glass before it tips and his hand wraps over mine, large and strong and heavy. "I think I can help you out, Ri."

I freeze, shooting him a look of disbelief. Whiplash seizes me and I stare at him, my mouth falling open. My heart hammers in my chest; my thoughts swirl in my head.

Torsten takes a deep breath, stares directly into my eyes, and says, "Marry me."

"What?" I gasp. I definitely heard him wrong. That's it. I've officially lost my mind. My wild and reckless has given way to *unhinged*.

Because there is no way in hell that Torsten Hansen, Norwegian sex god, just proposed to me at a corner diner in South Boston.

I blink slowly, trying to regulate my breathing. But when I meet Torsten's eyes again, he's still staring at me. His hand is still covering mine. His intensity is still dragging me under like quicksand.

He glances over his shoulder as the bells over the diner doors chime. Regulars begin to enter and Beth comes back from her break.

"Hear me out?" he murmurs, his voice low.

I nod, too confused to voice an objection.

"Sorry, Beth. Something came up. Any chance we can take these to go? I'll take the check."

"You got it." Beth sidles up next to our booth a few moments later with white Styrofoam containers and a bill. She gives me a long look that toes the line between uncertain and dislike.

Torsten pays while I fill the takeout containers with our pancakes.

"Let's go back to your place. We'll grab our cars later."

"Okay." I slip out of the booth, don my coat, and grab my purse. Torsten's fingers find the small of my back and guide me forward. I feel unsteady on my feet, in shock.

When he clears the door and we're back on the street, Torsten stops suddenly. "Rielle, wait."

I turn toward him, craning my neck so I can meet his eyes. "This is crazy," he blurts out, shoving his hands into his pockets. "I don't know what I was thinking. I—"

"I want to hear you out," I cut him off, surprising the hell out of both of us. I have no idea what Torsten's motivation is for proposing marriage but I'd be lying if I said I wasn't intrigued. Or a tiny bit hopeful. When I look at him, I see a soft place to land, a shoulder to lean on, a person who understands me on a deeper level. No matter how crazy his idea is, the fact that he wants to help me find a solution, is enough for me to want to listen.

He searches my eyes for a long moment before shaking his head. "Okay. Okay, we'll talk."

"We'll talk," I agree, falling in step beside him.

I walk beside her, wondering if I've lost my damn mind.

What the hell was I thinking? Did I seriously just propose marriage to a woman I've spent a total of fifteen hours with, in group settings, over blueberry pancakes?

Yes, yes I did.

We're quiet as we walk, both of us lost in our thoughts. Except mine swing from angry to needy to frustrated. I hate that Rielle questioned our friendship, as if I don't give a shit about her. I know we aren't close and don't really *know* each other but does she seriously think I treat her the same way I treat puck bunnies? Her accusation stung and it shouldn't have because it's the perception I've spent years cultivating.

I just don't like that it worked on *her*.

Then, there's the fact that she's obviously in some kind of trouble. Four hundred and seventy thousand dollars? Really? That's not normal credit card or student loan debt. That's serious, life-altering, damaging debt. Is someone trying to shake her down? Is that why she has bruises on her arm?

Jesus. I scrape a hand over my face, glancing at Rielle from the corner of my eye. She keeps her head straight ahead, her footsteps even, her shoulders pulled back. I couldn't get a read on her if I was a fucking mind reader.

But marriage? No, I didn't propose marriage. I proposed something different. *A transaction.* And she knows it.

The thought makes me feel cheap and dirty. I already feel like I fucked up by suggesting such an insane idea. But is it really that insane if it helps us both out? This way, I can get my papers to stay in the States and visit Farmor. And Rielle can get out of debt and search for a job she wants because of the role, not just the salary. It's like a different kind of friends-with-benefits agreement, right?

Way to rationalize that one, Hansen.

I take a fortifying breath and follow Rielle as she walks down a side street toward her apartment. I've escorted her home three times now and know this area pretty well. It's not the best part of town but seeing it with clearer eyes, in the morning light, with Rielle at my side, makes me wince. We pass a couple of drunk guys, sitting on a curb and passing a bottle back and forth. A woman digs through trash, her cheeks sunken and her expression gaunt.

Fuck. My chest aches that this is where Rielle lives. While I dine at The Ivy and order bespoke suits, this proud woman walking beside me has to step over broken glass and watch her back from men with roaming eyes and vulgar threats. The realization cuts me deep and I don't miss the way Rielle's shoulders round toward each other, as if she's protecting herself from the environment she currently lives in.

Who does she owe so much money to? Who laid hands on her?

We draw closer to her apartment building. Two men hanging in the parking lot stop and stare.

"You good, Rielle?" one of them calls out. He has a thick Southie accent.

Rielle lifts a hand and waves. "All good. Thanks, Merck."

He narrows his eyes, giving me a once-over. "You sure, girl? Because you don't have to—"

"I swear I'm fine!" Rielle hollers out, her cheeks blazing red.

I shoot the guy a look and trail after Rielle who seems to be speed walking toward the door.

"Who's that guy?" I ask her, dropping a hand to her shoulder.

She glances up at me, her eyes filled with shame. "That's Merck. The property manager."

"What did he mean—"

"He thinks I'm taking you back to my place to sleep with you. For…for money," she whispers.

"What the fuck?" I respond automatically, angrily. Dropping her arm, I turn toward the guys in the parking lot and take one step in their direction, practically vibrating with rage. How dare they think that about Rielle? How dare they think of her at all.

A surge of protectiveness mixed with jealousy I'm unprepared for blazes through me, propelling me forward.

"Wait. Torsten, please." Rielle hangs onto my arm, trying to pull me back.

I pause at the desperation in her tone.

When I glance at her, she looks near tears, even more so than last night, and it shocks me. Because in all the years I've known Rielle, I've never seen her actually cry. Not once. And I've seen Claire throw down more emotional outbursts than I can count.

I falter. "What is it?"

"Please. Just, come upstairs with me. Let's talk."

I narrow my eyes at her. "What they think—"

"It doesn't matter. Please don't make this more embarrassing for me. I'm so humiliated right now. And Merck, he doesn't mean it the way you think. He looks out for me. For real."

I scan her face before nodding once. Anger simmers in my veins as I follow her into the building and up the stairs. I note the smell of weed, the bickering behind closed doors, the screaming that rings out on floor three.

When we get to Rielle's door, she pulls a fresh pink slip off the doorframe and my stomach sinks as I recognize the eviction notice. My stomach twists so painfully, I think I'm going to be sick.

Rielle slips inside and I follow behind her, wincing at the sound the deadbolt makes when it slides into place.

"Want a water or something? We can finish our pancakes." She gestures toward her small kitchen table.

"Sure," I say, taking a seat just to put her at ease.

In truth, I'd rather pace her apartment like a caged lion demanding answers to all her fucking problems. Like why she's in so much debt. And why that man, Merck, thinks she'd sleep around for money. And why she hasn't told anyone about any of this. Because I know for a fact if Claire knew how rough things were for Rielle, she'd be living in the Merrick family home right now.

Rielle sets two glasses of water down and meets my gaze, a sheepish smile glancing off her lips. I realize I spoke my last thought aloud. "I didn't want anyone to know."

"Why, Ri? Not even Claire?"

"Especially not Claire." She sits down. "Her family—"

"Would have taken you in as theirs in a heartbeat."

She nods, a wistful look crossing her features before she blinks it away. "I'm not a charity case," she says, like she's reminding me.

"I know that."

"Do you?"

I heave a sigh and lean back in my chair. "Do you want to tell me about the debt?"

She shrugs. "Student loans."

"No way. Unless you went to Harvard, twice, you wouldn't be in that much debt."

She bites her bottom lip, her gaze darting out the window

before meeting my eyes once more. "My father and I had a falling out. A big one. I took out private loans for college, from a family friend. I wasn't as careful as I should have been when I read the terms." She frowns. "I trusted him, you know?"

I nod, because I do know. Only eight years ago, my father and uncle tried to change the terms of my trust. They would have succeeded if Farmor didn't realize what they were up to and put a stop to it.

"Anyway, his family hit some hard times and he changed the interest rate. So, here we are."

"Other than the student loans, what do you owe?"

"Nothing."

"Credit cards, medical, insurance policies?"

"Nope. Just the student loans. And my rent." She gestures to her apartment.

I nod, keeping my features schooled. Inside, I feel positively ill but Rielle is a proud woman. It's taking a lot for her to be open and honest with me right now. No way in hell am I going to say or do anything to make her feel like she can't be straight with me.

"Okay," I say, opening one of the takeout containers. I nudge the other one closer to her. She goes to the kitchen and returns with some cutlery. Once she's seated again, I meet her eyes. "Rielle, I'm not good at this stuff. I don't have a lot of practice with feelings and talking about them."

She smirks at me and for some reason, it's oddly encouraging.

"But," I continue, "I am good at dealing with complicated family members. I know what it's like to be underestimated and looked over by those you trust. No matter what goes down between us, don't ever think that I'm not your friend. I'm here for you. If you want to talk or not talk, whatever you need, I'm here. Okay?"

She stares at me for a long moment and some of the pain

in her expression eases, like air seeping out of a balloon. She nods.

"Okay." I smile.

"Will you tell me now why you proposed marriage as a solution to anything?"

I snort. "Yeah. Okay, I'm just going to be straight with you."

"I'd appreciate that."

I snicker, giving her a searching look. My humor fades as I grow serious. "I need a green card."

Rielle frowns. "What? Why? You're on the Hawks. You—"

"This is my last season. No one knows yet except for the owner, some senior management, and our coach." I shrug, keeping my voice light. "My body isn't holding up the way it used to."

Rielle's eyes widen and her mouth twists. "What do you mean? Are you injured?"

"I'm fine. It's just, time to hang up my skates. I've been in this country for a long time. I've built my life here, my future. I've started the application process twice to become a naturalized citizen but both times, I needed to head back to Oslo before the necessary paperwork was in order."

"You can't just pick up where you left off?"

I shake my head. "The process doesn't work that way."

"Well, why don't you just try again?"

I sigh, steepling my hands together. "I was going to. I mean, I still can. But my lawyer advised that if I start again, I need to stick around. And I can't make that commitment."

"But isn't this where you want to be?" She narrows her eyes. "Why can't you stick around?"

I roll my lips together and admit the truth. "My grandmother is ill."

"Oh." Rielle leans back in her seat, her expression thoughtful as she processes everything I'm saying. "So, you want to marry for the ability to stay in the US without having to go through the formal process that would restrict your movement?"

"Yes."

"And in exchange—"

"I'll pay off your loans. I'll provide you with a good lifestyle while you figure out your next steps. Whatever you need, you'll have. And you can take as much time as you need to find a job you love, one that doesn't burn you out."

She gasps. Disbelief ripples over her expression. "Just like that?"

"Yeah," I say, watching her carefully.

"Torsten"—she shakes her head—"I can't take advantage of your financial success like that."

I snort. "That's your takeaway? Rielle, you're not taking advantage of anything. I'm taking advantage of your situation to try to circumvent the system."

She wrinkles her nose and looks adorable. Innocent. It's a glimpse of the girl behind the woman and it makes me smile, even though I'm in the middle of the most serious conversation I've ever had.

"Are you serious?" she asks.

"I am if you are. But, you have to know, this is illegal."

She chuckles and I lean forward, drawn to whatever she's going to say next. "Torsten, I spent the first eighteen years of my life following every rule you can think of. It left me miserable and hurt. Since then, I've broken a bunch just to survive. Trust me, I'm not judging you. *Stan*."

I snicker. "So, you're in?" My heart hammers in my eardrums.

She nods slowly, giving me another one of her smiles. "With conditions. But yes, I'm in."

"Okay," I whisper, grinning like a lunatic. "Tell me about your conditions."

She lifts a shoulder and lets it drop. "More like

hammering out logistics. You can't just bankroll my entire life."

I laugh. That's what she's worried about? Me paying for her lifestyle? "Okay, sweetheart. We'll discuss details in a minute. But first, I want you to know that I can make this work for both of us. We're friends, right?"

She nods.

"And I trust you, Ri. More than I trust most people."

"I trust you too," she says.

"Good." I smile. Rielle smiles back and it's like a storm cloud receding, making way for sunshine. Her brilliance shines through and blinds me. Because when Rielle smiles, she dazzles.

I slip from my chair and get down on one knee beside her. Grinning up at her, I don't care how goofy I am. Because I'm going to do this the right way. It's most likely the only time I'll ever do it and I'm already off to a shaky start.

"Rielle Carter, will you marry me?"

She rolls her eyes but a giggle escapes her throat. "Yes, Torsten. I'll marry you."

 Marrying NHL legend Torsten Hansen may seem like a crazy idea but it's a hell of a lot better than living in an alleyway, begging Claire for her family's help, or, the worst-case scenario, calling Dad and apologizing for choosing my own path in life. Torsten's proposal may be surprising but it's hardly *bad*.

As I stare into his deep blue eyes and get a glimpse of that dimple, it doesn't feel as insane as it should. It feels…hopeful. Like a new beginning.

Shacked up in my dilapidated apartment, agreeing to a marriage proposal with no ring, from a man I didn't even consider a *friend* last week, should have me running for Merck. Instead, I feel relaxed, even a little bit excited.

This is an amazing solution to everything.

Torsten will get his green card and be able to stay in the US. I'll pay back Jerry Jensen without the lingering fear of having to crawl back to Dad. And our marriage will be a business agreement.

Arrangements and deals I can do. Relationships and giving up my freedom, I cannot.

We'll have an agreement, a contract. One that I'll have a lawyer—Indy's best friend Aiden Hardsin comes to mind—

look over. In a few years, I'll be divorced, with a couple of years of work experience under my belt, a savings account, and my whole future in front of me.

Sure, it's not the life I envisioned for myself. But all those old *fairy tales*—you know, happily-ever-afters and riding off into the sunset—fell in my rearview mirror the night I left Dad's house. Since then, I've been focused on creating my own financial stability. On surviving.

I glance at Torsten. He seems relaxed too, as if the weight of the world is no longer hanging around his neck. His eyes are brighter, his grin wider, his tone softer.

"This is fantastic." I smile at him.

He chuckles and shakes his head. "It is?"

I nod and eat a bite of pancakes. "You were right. These are phenomenal," I tell him, eating another forkful. "Now, let's talk terms."

"Terms," he repeats. "Your conditions?"

"Yeah. We need to hammer out all the details up front so there aren't any surprises down the road."

"Right." He nods, his eyes dimming a bit. "That's a good idea."

"We marry for, how long? One year, two?"

"Two at a minimum."

Two years. I'm nearly twenty-five. I'll be divorced at twenty-seven. For a second, the realization leaves my stomach feeling funny, like it's another failure to add to the top of my stack. But that's ridiculous, right? I'm not setting out to make this marriage work, it's only a *contract*, so it's not going to fail. It's just going to end, the way it's intended to.

Marriages of convenience fulfill a purpose and once Torsten and I fulfill ours, we *should* move on.

"You'll move into my place," Torsten says.

"Okay," I agree, thinking over the logistics. Will I have my own room? Or share his? I try to envision Torsten's bedroom and a masculine, moody, all dark wood and light gray, floats into my mind.

"What's wrong?"

"Huh?" I clear my head.

"You just made a face." He points at me, his expression growing serious. "You know we need to show that we're a real couple, a couple in love, in order for you to sponsor me. We have to get married, take pictures, have a celebration, live together, and document it all. You're going to be my wife, Rielle," Torsten says slowly.

"Your wife," I repeat, a little dazed by the term. It slams into me like a grenade, blowing up the life I've been grinding for up until this point. All of my worries, about the loans, about my rent, about buying another super pack of ramen noodles, are going to cease to exist. They won't even register on my radar.

A flame of panic burns through me for a second. The water I've been treading grows choppy and a few waves slap me in the face. Because holy shit, I'm going to marry a professional hockey player who has enough money to pay off my loan. Enough money to take my freedom, curtail my choices, *control* me.

I jump from the chair and begin to pace. For some strange reason, my reaction causes Torsten to relax even more. Was he waiting for an emotional outburst? Was he worried by how calmly I was taking it all?

Maybe he should be.

Because he is a man with money and means. I grew up raised in a circle of men like that and none of them turned out to be as trustworthy, as honest, as decent as they pretended. Sure, they looked the part, they even *acted* it, but away from prying eyes and whispering mouths, lurked something a hell of a lot more sinister.

Torsten's presence, his huge frame coupled with his larger-than-life personality draw my attention. My heart rate hammers and my breathing accelerates as his gaze holds mine. Ice blue to charcoal black. His gaze is heated, his expression intense. I feel drawn to him, a moth to a flame, a damaged soul to a compassionate one.

The next realization rolls over me like a tidal wave. I *like* Torsten Hansen. I have real *feelings* for him. Maybe they're shallow ones but given enough time, given the circumstances, they could grow into a black hole, one that swallows me up completely. My breathing stutters in my chest and I dig the heel of my hand to the center of my breastbone.

Torsten catches the movement and concern rings his irises. He leans forward in his chair, ready to spring into action if I need him.

And I do. I have. For five years, I didn't rely on anyone but myself until now. Until him.

"Torsten, I can't live with you."

"What? Why not?"

I draw in a shaky breath. "I, well, for starters, I could never afford half your rent." I grasp at straws, especially since he already informed me he was taking over all the financial aspects of our life together.

At that, he tosses his head back and laughs. It's a deep, rumbly laugh. One that starts in his stomach and causes his chest to vibrate. It makes goosebumps break out on my skin and my stomach clench because it's also the sexiest laugh I've ever heard in my life.

And Torsten Hansen, with his golden hair and brilliant blue eyes, with his muscled torso and his strong shoulders, looks incredibly sexy doing it.

I freeze. Watching Torsten laugh, I realize my assumptions are correct. Marrying him isn't a problem at all. It's the extricating myself from our marriage that's going to destroy me.

"We need boundaries," I blurt out.

"Boundaries?" he repeats, wiping the tears from his eyes.

I nod and continue my pacing. He watches me with amusement that unsettles me further.

"For example, I'll need my own bedroom."

"Absolutely," he agrees, sobering when he notes how serious I am.

I force myself to sit back down but push the pancakes away. Tucking my hair behind my ears, I let out a shaky breath and ask the question that's tearing me up the most. "What about dating?"

Torsten's amusement slips away entirely.

The gravity of what we're agreeing to smacks us both in the face. Of course he'd be concerned about dating. He's an NHL legend with legions of fans and a female following that rivals his male worshippers. For me, it's a non-issue. I don't date. I have one-night stands with no promises, no goodbyes, and absolutely no emotions involved.

He clears his throat. "Tell me what you're thinking. What you want?"

I tap my fingertips against my lips. I think about us living together, about women with toned bodies and long, blonde hair flouncing out of his bedroom in the morning, giving me a pitying look. My chest squeezes painfully. I hate the idea of Torsten with other women. Not that I can tell him that. Instead, I settle on a safe, logical objection. "I don't want to look stupid. I mean, if we're married and you're out and—"

"It won't happen," he cuts me off. "We have to do this the right way or not at all."

I raise my eyebrows at him. "You're going to marry me for *two years* and forgo sex?"

He stares at me for a long moment. His gaze searching, his eyes hard. "I'll be faithful to you, Ri. I won't step out on you. You won't find yourself in any compromising situations. When I give my word, I mean it. I'm taking vows and even though it's not for the right reasons, we'll be husband and wife."

Surprise rushes through me. I fall into the bottomless pools of Torsten's eyes. He's *serious*. My fingers tremble at the intensity in his expression, my heart rate spikes at the truth in his voice. My entire body tightens and hums with an awareness, an approval, that is too hard to ignore.

We'll be husband and wife.

I smile at him. He smiles back. And my world tilts a little bit on its axis, making me question everything I thought I knew about Torsten Hansen, Hawks heartbreaker and perpetual bachelor.

I force my attention back to the conversation. This is still a negotiation and when you make emotional decisions, you end up on the losing side. I clear my throat. "Okay, good. So, separate bedrooms, no cheating, anything else? I'm happy to sign a prenup, obviously. You'll be traveling with the team over the next two months so we'll have a chance to settle in without everything being awkward."

Torsten blows out an exhale and leans back in his chair. He raps his knuckles against the table. "I'll have my lawyer draw everything up. I'll hire you a lawyer too or you can just send me the bill for whoever you're most comfortable working with. There's one more thing we need to discuss."

"What?" I narrow my eyes.

"What are we going to tell people? Obviously, we can't really share our story or we'll end up—"

"In jail," I snort.

Torsten takes a gulp of his water. "Exactly. But, there's no way we can pull this off without being honest with Easton and Claire."

"Or Indy and Noah," I mutter, knowing he's right.

"Austin," he adds. "I'll talk to the guys before our team meeting tonight. We're going over video reels."

"Okay. I'll message Claire and Indy and see if we can meet for coffee." I tap my fingers against the table, thinking of all the ways this is going to blow up in my face. There's no way in hell that Claire's feelings aren't going to be hurt when she realizes the scheme I'm about to pull off. She won't buy that I'm just getting married to help out Torsten. Besides, I can't tell her he's not re-signing because the team doesn't know yet. Shit, am I going to lose my best friend's trust?

"What is it?" Torsten asks.

I lick my lips. "I don't know what to tell Claire."

His expression softens. "We'll tell them a variation of the truth. That six weeks ago, I helped you home after you drank your face off with Claire."

"That's true."

"Yeah."

"And that we've been talking since then. Hanging out as friends."

"As friends," he agrees. "And that when I mentioned my predicament to you, you offered to help me out because—"

"Because I needed out of my job. Away from my boss."

He narrows his eyes. "Don't think we're not going to address what really happened last night."

I lower my gaze.

"Just tell me, Ri. Who bruised you up? Someone related to the loan, your ex-boss? I need to know. I need to make sure whoever the hell he is, he won't ever put his hands on you again."

I sigh. "It was Stu, my ex-boss. But we don't have time to get into everything right now." I flick my wrist, desperate to keep us on track. "I'll explain to Claire that I agreed to move in with you and take some time to explore my career path without the financial pressure I'm under. I mean, Claire and Indy know I have loans. They just don't know the whole story."

"What is the whole story?" he tries again.

I flash him a quick grin. "Not going there, Torst."

"Ri, I'm in the middle of playoffs. My contract is up at the end of June. In order for this to work, it's going to happen fast. Real fast."

"Okay," I agree.

He searches my eyes, as if looking for confirmation to match my words. "So, we have a deal?"

I take a deep breath and look around my shitty apartment. When my eyes latch onto Torsten's again, I nod. "We have a deal."

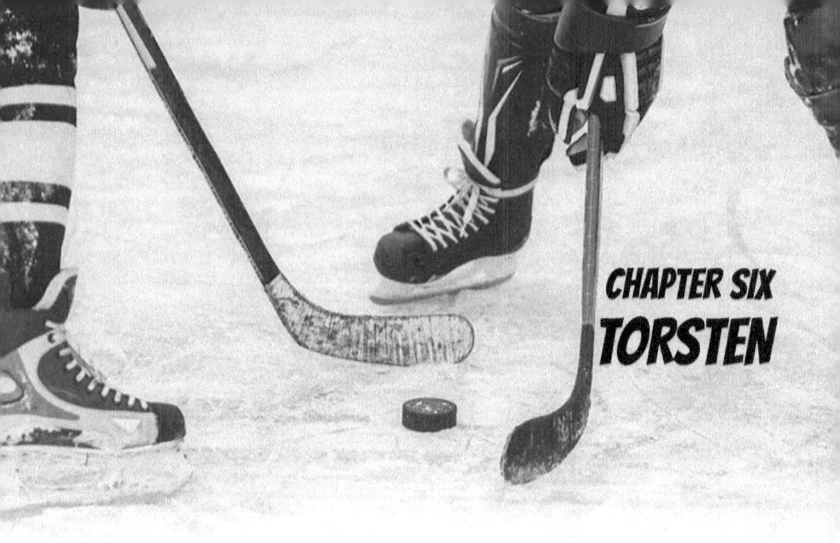

I wasn't kidding when I told Rielle we'd have to move fast. By the end of the night, I've confided in my closest friends and teammates, bought Rielle a ring, and scanned the papers Bill sent over. I'm changing into sweats for the night, when I glance at the clock. It's nearing midnight and Rielle still isn't home.

You're not her keeper.

Still, a flicker of worry flares in my chest. I still don't know the full story about her student loans. I don't know the full story with the fuckhead ex-boss who touched her. I don't know any of Rielle's full stories and I have no clue where she is. With each minute that passes, my nerves jump and my concern increases.

What am I doing? Two nights ago, I didn't think twice about Rielle Carter unless I was picturing her plump lips closing over my cock and how sweet it would feel to sink inside of her. Now, I'm stressed because a handful of hours have passed and she hasn't checked in.

Is this what marriage is like? Constantly worrying about someone?

I sigh and tug on my sweatpants. Pausing, I take in my room, as if I'm seeing it through new eyes. The mahogany furniture, the sturdy, boxy bed frame, the gray and black comforter. Everything about it screams bachelor and for years, I reveled in that. But now, I wish it was a little softer. I wish it had a woman's touch. *Rielle's.*

I'm reaching for my T-shirt when the apartment door latch catches. I hear a burst of giggling. Grinning to myself, I toss my clothes in the hamper and make my way out of my bedroom.

Then, I freeze. Because Rielle is standing in the center of the living room. Her arms are raised over her head, her expression, cast in moonlight, is dreamy. Her eyes are closed, her body swaying to whatever music she's turning over in her mind.

But that body. I work a swallow. She's dressed in skintight leather pants and a cropped top. The sexiest boots I've ever seen mold over her knees. Her hair is a wild tangle of curls, tumbling down her back.

She must feel my gaze because she stops moving and turns to glance at me over her shoulder.

Black eyes that glint and burn. A lush mouth that's sinful in its ability to tempt. Curves my hands are desperate to feel. My throat dries, my eyes widen, and I take a tentative step closer.

"Rielle." My voice is raspy, deep.

Rielle grins and it hits me straight in the chest. "Hello, soon-to-be *husband.*"

Husband. It's the one word I focus on and I like the way it sounds coming from her mouth. A hell of a lot more than I'm supposed to.

I grin and close the space between us. She's obviously tipsy. "How much did you drink?"

"More than I meant to." She wrinkles her nose and it's adorable.

"You know we were supposed to look over papers tonight, right?"

She nods, her mouth pushing into a pout. "I know. And I swear I didn't set out for this."

"Trouble just finds you?" I tease.

She winces. "It's a byproduct of being best friends with Claire."

I laugh and sit down on the couch. Even though I shouldn't, I pull her into my lap. She doesn't shift to move away so I wrap my arms around her casually. "How did Claire take the news?"

"Not very well," she whispers, her expression serious.

Shit. My heart sinks a little at her words.

"Hence the drinks," she adds.

I nod, frowning.

"But once I told her the full story about Stu, she came around."

"I still want the full story about Stu."

She blushes and dips her head. "After we talked, she insisted on an impromptu bachelorette. Indy was our DD."

Of course she did. Claire Merrick is the life of any and every party. But she's also a loyal friend, protective and caring of those she loves. And I know she adores Rielle. Some of my worry recedes knowing Claire is supporting Ri in this decision.

Rielle's hand trails down my bare torso, her touch light.

"You definitely don't look thirty-seven," she murmurs.

I chuckle, fighting the urge to flex for her like a twenty-year-old punk. "That's cause I'm practically thirty-eight."

She snorts.

"We can look at the papers and sign tomorrow morning. I have to be at the arena at two for a team meeting and to get ready for our game tomorrow night. If all looks good, we'll be getting hitched in two days. Right before I leave for Tampa."

Her eyes snap up to mine, wide and brimming with more emotion than she usually shows.

"You really want to be my husband, Torst?"

She asks the question softly, as if she's unsure of the answer. As if she wants the answer to mean more than just some contract we both sign. And God, I want it to mean more than that too.

I nod, not trusting my voice. I clear my throat. "I like the way that sounds more than I should." My fingers swipe over her hip, my hand palming her thigh.

She shifts her weight so she can wrap her arms around my neck. "I shouldn't like that you like it as much as I do."

My eyebrows lift and I smile. Her hands slide down the back of my neck and palm my shoulders. I sit perfectly still as her fingers explore my arms, my upper back, before wrapping back around my neck.

The space between us hums with awareness that wasn't there earlier. It's potent and intense and could be goddamn electrifying if we gave into its pull.

"How much have you had to drink?"

She shakes her head, the ends of her hair tickling my hand. "Not nearly enough. I can hold my liquor."

"I'm learning that, sweetheart."

I watch as her eyelids drop to half-mast. My breathing ticks up a notch. My fingers slide up from her thigh, over her hip, until I can touch the exposed skin of her lower back. I flirt with the waistband of her leggings, dipping the edges beneath the leather until I graze the lace of her thong.

I need to stop touching her. Right now. Five seconds ago. My hand stills.

We're making an agreement. We're signing a contract.

Nowhere in it does it include *this*. An attraction that is gripping in its intensity, desperate in its need.

Rielle leans forward, her chest colliding with mine. "Rielle." Her name is a plea on my lips. It comes out protective and concerned, tender and caring, and all the things in between.

"Are you going to kiss me at the altar?" she asks, her voice so throaty I feel it everywhere.

"Do you want me to?" My hand slides lower, until my palm molds to her ass. I squeeze and she gasps. "Tell me."

Slowly, she nods. And fuck, I want to kiss her at the altar. Right now, I want it to already be our wedding day. So I can meet her at the altar, kiss her senseless, carry her over the goddamn threshold, and give her a proper wedding night. But that's the kind of dangerous thinking that will set us up for trouble down the road.

"Then we should practice," she murmurs.

"Fuck, sweetheart. You're making this hard." My hand not currently down her pants cups the side of her neck and slides up to her cheek. I angle her head with one hand to stare into her eyes. Hunger and need spark with desire and I groan, already hard and thick and pressing into her.

She shifts closer and reaches for me, her eyes boring into mine, holding me captive.

I swear and lose my restraint. My mouth arcs down and she closes her eyes just as my lips touch hers. I kiss her hard, with purpose. With intent. Once, twice, and then, my tongue slips inside her mouth and I kiss her with unbridled want.

Her arms wrap all the way around my neck and she pulls herself up my body, our chests pressed together. My hand resting against her ass grips hard until she twists in my lap and straddles me. Our exchange morphs, turning needy and borderline desperate. My mouth drags from her lips to her neck. My hand slides lower, my fingertips slipping under the material of her thong to tease her core.

I swear. She's so fucking wet for me. She wants this as much as I do and yet... "Tell me you want this, Ri."

She digs her nails into my back. "I want you, Torsten." As soon as she says the words, I'm moving us through the kitchen and into my bedroom.

I drop her in the center of my bed and step back, just to admire her, to remember this moment.

I hold her gaze as she works her crop top over her head. I rock back on my heels when her breasts bounce free. She's not even wearing a bra.

I grip her ankles and pull until she's lying flat on my bed. Then, I slowly unzip her sexy boots and tug them off her feet. Next, I roll down the leather leggings, inch by inch. They're so goddamn tight, they could be a second skin.

My breathing ticks up, my eyes scanning her body and trying to memorize every dip and curve. Trying to track it all like she's suddenly going to disappear.

When she's spread out beneath me in nothing but a black lace thong, I drink her in, knowing it will never be enough. "You're the most beautiful woman I've ever had the pleasure of seeing, of knowing, Rielle." The words are quiet but I mean them. I don't say things like this to women. I never lead them on, never make promises I can't keep. I just search and hope and wish for more. Now, Rielle is granting me the more and dammit, it means something even though it's not supposed to. "I mean it. There's no one like you."

Tenderness blazes through her eyes, intense and heady and sincere. She reaches out, her fingertips brushing against the tops my shoulders but I step back. "I have something for you."

She frowns, leaning up onto her elbows. Nervous energy zips through my body. Rielle is practically naked in my bed and I'm the one who feels vulnerable, whose heart is about to beat out of my chest. I reach into the top drawer of my dresser and remove the small pouch containing her ring.

She watches me, mesmerized, as my big fingers fumble with the strings. I laugh again. "I tied it too tightly. I was nervous I'd lose it before I had a chance to give it to you."

She sits straight up, her eyes wide, her mouth dropping open.

I drop to my knees for the second time in her presence and take her hand in mine. "We're doing this all backwards. But I don't care because our story is quickly becoming my favorite."

She draws in a sharp inhale, her fingers trembling in mine.

I wish I knew what she's thinking. I wish I knew if I was scaring the hell out of her or if she was pleased or pitying me for being so goddamn emotional over a contract. But when I gaze into Rielle's eyes, everything that passes between us feels like more than just an agreement. Fine, it may not be happily-ever-after and stars and rainbows, but it's real.

It's mine and hers.

I work a swallow and forge ahead. "Rielle Carter, I know this isn't a traditional love story. I know we have an expiration date and are jumping into this for less than honest reasons." The corner of her mouth tugs up and for one blink, she looks more like a wishful girl than a fierce woman. "But I swear to you, I will respect and cherish you always, even when you're no longer mine. I admire your strength, am in awe of your courage, and feel both small and tall in your presence. Thank you for agreeing to marry me." I slip the ring on her finger.

She gasps as she holds out her hand and admires the diamond on the ring finger of her left hand. It's elegant—a two-carat diamond in a princess cut, with a thin platinum band. I hold my breath, waiting for her reaction, hoping like hell she likes it.

"I love it. It's beautiful," she says, looking up at me. "You picked the perfect ring."

I smile, relief unspooling through my limbs. "I picked the perfect girl."

She wrinkles her nose at my being so corny and I laugh. But I still mean it. I've dated scores of women and none of them have come close to Ri. "Now..." I shift until I'm hovering over her. She lays back against the mattress as I crawl up her body. "I'm going to make you scream my name, sweetheart. But I'm saving sex for our wedding night." I drop a kiss to her forehead, then her nose, her lips.

"What?" she snorts, her thighs clenching together. "After that speech and this ring"—she holds up her hand—"you're going to make me wait for it?"

"Promise, I'll make it so good for you," I swear, dragging the tip of my nose along her jawline. I nip at her earlobe and my hand finds her breast, massaging it.

She whimpers, arching into me.

"And after you say 'I do,' if you still want this, with me, I'll light you up, babe. But if we get one thing right, it's going to be our wedding night." I pull back to look at her and note the vulnerability in her expression. I feel it reflected in mine and admit the truth. "You're the only woman I'll ever marry, Rielle. And call me old-fashioned but the wedding night..."

"You want a traditional one?" she whispers.

I nod, feeling a blush work over my cheeks. Jesus, I'm the goddamn blushing bride in this arrangement.

She laughs but then shakes her head. "Your logic is endearing, Torsten." She bites her bottom lip. "You're much more romantic than I thought you'd be."

I chuckle and slide my palm down her body. "But we can still play tonight. If you want."

She slips her hand up my arm and around my back, bringing my lips to hers. She kisses me hard. Deep. "I'd like that," she whispers, right as my fingers dip under the material of the scrap of lace between her legs.

I breathe out a tortured sigh. "How long have you been this wet for me, Ri?"

"Since I was getting ready to go out tonight," she admits, her words unleashing a torrent of lust through my veins. I push one, then two, fingers inside of her and swear.

The sound of her arousal mixed with our panting is the only sound in the room for several long seconds. It turns her on even more and I'm painfully hard, more desperate for her touch than for my next breath.

"Lie back, baby. Let me take care of you," I murmur.

She does as I say but shakes her head. "Let me see you, Torsten."

My eyes are already sinking closed. Slowly, I drag my fingers away from her and shed my sweatpants. My cock springs free, ready to fucking burst. She draws in a sharp inhale and licks her lips.

Fuck. I hold her eyes as I pump my hand over my shaft, using her arousal as lube. Her eyes are hooded, the tip of her tongue swiping over her bottom lip. She's so goddamn sexy, such a fucking temptress.

I can't tear my eyes away as she brings her hands up to her bare breasts and touches herself, never dragging her gaze away from my hand wrapped around myself.

"Fuck," I murmur. "This is going to be harder than I thought."

"No pun intended," she breathes out.

I snort and move back to the bed. I pull her body to the edge of the mattress and dip down to my knees. Then, I hook her thighs over my shoulders and push her thong to the side.

She arches off the bed, her eyes closing in anticipation of what's coming.

She shivers as I blow on her sensitive flesh. Right before my mouth pleasures her, I admit, "If we're not careful, I'm going to think this is for real, Rielle."

Then my mouth covers her and she bucks off the bed.

She never responds to my confession and I'm not sure if I'm relieved or disappointed by her silence.

CHAPTER SEVEN
TORSTEN

I wake up early the morning of my wedding day. Pale light filters in through the window of my bedroom. I never pulled the blackout shades down last night.

My sheets are twisted around my legs and instinctively, I reach for Rielle even though she's sleeping in the guest room. Two nights ago, we crossed every single boundary but one. Yesterday, we signed all the formal paperwork. Today, we're getting married. And I'm desperate to finally be inside of her tonight, when she's mine, with a wedding band on her finger.

An ache throbs behind my ribs. While I know today is a sham, in many ways it feels so real. Too real. Especially after the other night. Hearing Rielle moan my name, watching her break apart under my fingers, my mouth, changes things. There's no way I can keep my distance for two goddamn years. It scares me to think that even now, I already don't want to let her go when our agreement comes to an end.

My phone buzzes on my nightstand and I frown when I see Farmor's name on the screen. Swiping to answer, I relocate to the living room.

"Farmor? Everything okay?" I ask.

Her breathy laugh floats through the line. "Does something have to be wrong for me to call my favorite grandson?"

she responds, her Norwegian crisp and rapid. Even though she's nearly ninety and in poor health, she'd never intentionally let you know it.

"Of course not. How are you?" I flip on the coffee pot. Last year, I bought one of those fancy, overpriced espresso machines but I still haven't figured out how to use it. While I wait for the coffee to brew, I slide onto a barstool. "Farmor?"

"I'm still here, Torsten. And I'm fine. Getting up there in years, but fine."

I smile. "What would you like to chat about?"

She stalls and worry runs through my veins. Is it cancer? Did something happen to my father? Anders? What—

"I've been doing some thinking," she says finally.

"Okay."

"About the promise you made me."

I close my eyes and let out a shaky breath. The day I left for America, barely nineteen and with a chip the size of Asia on my shoulder, I made Farmor a promise that has kept me awake on multiple occasions. "I remember."

"It's time, Torsten," she says gently. Tears prick the corners of my eyes because if it's *time*, that means Farmor knows she doesn't have much time left with us. She's dying and she knows it.

"I'm getting married today," I tell her.

She sputters for a moment and then, laughter. Real, genuine laughter that causes me to chuckle even though a tear drops to my cheek at the same time. I scrub it away with the back of my hand.

"You didn't tell me you were serious with someone," she prods.

"It happened quickly," I say, sticking to as much of the truth as possible.

"She's American?"

"Yes."

"So you're planning to stay?" I hear the hurt in her tone

and I have to swallow past the lump in my throat. Deep down, I know Farmor truly believed that if I come home to Norway, make amends with my father, he'll bring me back into our family business. She's always thought of my time in America as a phase, as an exploration of sorts, but never my future.

Never my legacy.

And now, as much as it pains me, I admit, "Yes. I'm planning to stay."

She's quiet for a long minute. She clears her throat and when she speaks, her words are devoid of judgement. "But you'll still come?"

"I'll come," I agree, relieved that I made the right decision in marrying Rielle. I knew at some point, Farmor would call and I'd need to go home. Because while my entire family has forsaken me and in many ways, I've turned my back on them, it never applied to Farmor and me. Our relationship is the most consistent, stable one in my life. Whatever she asks, I'll do. She knows it which is why she never asks the impossible of me, always just shy of it.

"Bring your bride, Torsten."

Surprise rocks through me at the request. "You want to meet Rielle?"

"Of course. She's becoming a Hansen, isn't she?"

The lump in my throat expands until it nearly chokes me. "Yeah," I manage.

"Okay. I'll see you soon, then. *Bryllupskort!*" She adds her congratulations to the happy couple and ends the call.

"Shit," I mutter, standing from the barstool. Before I can turn toward the coffee pot, Rielle steps into the kitchen.

Dressed in sleep shorts that barely cover her ass and a baggy T-shirt, with her hair tangled and trailing down her back, she looks exquisite. I drink her in greedily, wishing I could escort her to my bed to finish everything we started the other night. Soon enough.

Instead, I grin. "Coffee?"

She nods, her eyes still heavy with sleep. She steps toward the kitchen island, her bare legs calling to me like a siren I can't tear my eyes away from. Eventually, after an awkward amount of time passes, I succeed and pour two cups of coffee.

Rielle leans over the kitchen island and blows on her coffee.

"What're you thinking, Ri?" I stand on the opposite side of the island and watch her. Does she regret the other night? Signing all the papers yesterday? Coming to my game and sitting with the WAGs last night? Does she not want to marry me today? If she does, would she want to go to Norway?

She looks up and a grin lifts one side of her mouth. "It's our wedding day." Her voice is calm and strong. Not filled with nerves or second thoughts.

It settles me some and I smile back. "You're going to make a beautiful bride."

She wrinkles her nose and laughs. "Does it all feel a little too…real?"

I nod, reaching across the island to wrap the ends of her hair around my fingers. It's hard to be near Rielle and not touch her. Is this normal? "I like it though."

"Me too. Who were you on the phone with?"

I glance at my phone on the island. "My grandmother. Farmor."

"Oh." Surprise colors her tone as she lifts her mug and takes a sip of coffee. Her eyes flutter closed. "Caffeine is my drug of choice."

I snort.

"How's your grandma?" She opens her eyes.

"I know this is a lot considering we're getting married in a few hours—"

"Is she coming?" Horror washes over Rielle's face.

"No, not at all. She's in Norway," I reassure her,

wondering why it would be so terrible if Farmor crashed our wedding.

"Thank God," Rielle murmurs. "I know this"—she gestures between us—"is a massive lie. And I'm okay with it. But to have to lie to a sweet, little old lady just feels…wrong."

My stomach sinks at the conviction in her voice. There's no way she's going to want to go to Norway. But how the hell would I explain her absence to Farmor? She'd see through any bullshit reason I gave.

"What is it? What's wrong?" Rielle asks.

I lean back, startled. Did she read me that easily? "Nothing."

"Nope." She shakes her head. "You smushed your lips together."

I snort. "I did not."

"You did." She nods vigorously. "It's your tell."

I laugh and shake my head. "I don't have a tell."

"You do. Now, tell me what's wrong. We're getting married at noon and hair and makeup and Claire are going to be here any minute. If there's something you need to say, then—"

"Do you have a passport?"

"What? Yes."

"Have you ever been to Norway?"

Her eyes widen, recognition flaring in their black depths. "Why?" she asks slowly.

"I'm going to assume that we're going to the Finals, that we're going to win the Cup."

She grins but her eyebrows dip in confusion.

"Afterwards, this summer, do you want to meet a not-so-sweet, little old lady?" I grin.

Rielle swears just as a knock sounds on the door. She moves to answer it, bringing her coffee with her.

The second she pulls open the door, mayhem ensues. Claire leads a freaking calvary into the space. There're two women with massive trunks, a man wheeling in a dress rack filled with wedding gowns, and someone carrying a director's chair and a light.

"What's happening?" I ask, striding into the room, my coffee forgotten.

Claire gasps and clutches at her neck. "What are you doing here? You can't see her!" She jabs a finger in Rielle's direction. "It's bad luck."

I frown, ready to inform Claire that she's taking this whole thing too far but then Rielle giggles. She giggles and I see the excitement in her expression. Her eyes soften, her mouth curls into a smile, and she even bounces on her toes.

I hold up my hands in surrender. "What do you need me to do?"

Claire grins. "Good answer, Big Daddy. Your husband game is strong."

Rielle snorts. Indy comes barreling through the door, loaded with a massive brown paper bag. "I got bagels and all the spreads!"

"Champagne?" Claire asks over her shoulder.

"Duh," Indy responds. "Everyone knows mimosas are a staple for the bride on the morning of her wedding." She plops the bag down on my dining table and looks up. Then, she gasps and glares at me. "You need to leave."

"He knows," Claire reassures her.

Rielle glances at me, laughter and amusement in her eyes.

"I'm going, I'm going." I move toward my bedroom.

"Pack up whatever you need," Indy instructs me as she taps on her phone screen.

I enter my bedroom and hear her call after me. "Noah will be here in ten minutes to collect you."

"To collect me?" I pop my head out of my bedroom.

The three girls and even the makeup artists and hair stylist glare at me.

"Chop chop." Claire claps her hands.

"Don't forget the rings," Indy reminds me.

I laugh and move around my room, collecting everything I need. Less than ten minutes later, Claire is hustling me out the door. At the last moment, I turn to find Rielle. When our eyes collide, I smile. "See you at City Hall?"

She nods, tenderness sweeping her expression. "I'll be the one in white."

I chuckle, she smiles, and I have to fight the urge to stride across the room and kiss her in front of the entire circus unfolding in my living room.

Instead, Claire pushes me through the door and I reluctantly meet Noah.

I IMAGINE THAT BLOODY MARYS, pancakes and eggs, and Xbox with the guys is less exciting than whatever Rielle's getting into with her girlfriends.

"Dude, that's the fifth time you checked your watch," Panda, our team goalie, calls me out.

I slip my hand in my pocket.

"You nervous?" Easton asks.

"No. I just, I'm ready."

"To get married?" Skepticism is still heavy in Panda's voice. For years, Panda, Easton, and I were the Hawks who shut down clubs and got lost inside of women whose names we couldn't recall the next morning. Then, Easton went to rehab and started dating Claire. Now, I'm getting married. By the confusion in Panda's tone, I can tell he's trying to keep up with the sudden changes and figure out who the hell is going to wingman him now.

I turn toward him but James, the other Hawks defenseman and one of my oldest friends, says, "When you know, you know. And when that happens, you don't want to waste one more second without your woman tucked under your arm."

I shoot him a grateful smile, happy he decided to come today. James's wife passed about a year ago and I can't imagine how difficult it is for him to attend weddings and recall his own trip down the aisle. I was nothing short of grateful when he walked into Easton's Beacon Hill brownstone with a grin on his face, dressed in a sharp suit, holding a flower box with a boutonniere inside.

"Okay, boys," Noah announces. "It's time for us to head to City Hall. Let's get Big Daddy hitched!"

Easton whistles loudly, James claps, and even Panda grins at me.

Emotions I'm unprepared for wash over me. I remind myself that this isn't real, that Rielle isn't my forever woman, that today is a means to an end.

But as I follow my friends out to the parking lot, I can't ignore the excitement that thrums in my veins, the expectation that hums in my temples, or the happiness that grips my heart.

Today, I marry Rielle Carter.

My wedding dress is stunning. It's exquisite. It's exactly what I would have chosen if I was marrying for love, for real, and by the tears in Claire's eyes, she knows it too.

"You look breathtaking, Rielle," Indy whispers, tucking some flowers into my hair.

The stylists have all left, the penthouse is in disarray, and Claire and I polished off a bottle of champagne. Right now, it's just the three of us, and the last year with all of its ups and downs, laughter and tears, triumphs and failures, slams into me as I meet their eyes in the reflection of the mirror. My friendships with these two women have been the one constant I counted on for the past year.

Now, today, I'll be adding Torsten to that number. For two years, at least.

My stomach sours when I think of our expiration date.

"What's wrong?" Claire frowns.

I shake my head, shake away the thoughts that don't matter because today is my wedding day. "Nothing." My hands smooth over my hair one last time. It's been curled into big waves that cascade over my shoulders. The front pieces have been pulled back and blue hydrangeas hold it all together.

"Something blue," Indy explains when my fingers delicately trace a petal.

I smile. "Do you guys think this is too much?" I tilt my head, studying my curve-hugging dress. The top is all lace, with capped sleeves and scalloped edges that dip low in the front. A huge lace band binds my waist before fanning out into delicate tulle that falls straight to the floor. I lift the skirt to peek at my heels, incredible Manolo Blahnik white satin pumps with a peep toe. A wedding gift from my besties.

Indy shakes her head as Claire nods. We all burst out laughing.

"It's definitely too much for City Hall," Claire explains, waving her arms up and down the length of my body. "You're going to draw a lot of attention and turn a lot of heads. Just the way we like it!"

I laugh, nodding in agreement.

"But," Indy adds, "we still thought it would be fun to go all out and have a real wedding day."

"It is," I agree, turning toward her. "Everything happened so quickly with Torsten, so unexpectedly. I can't believe the team flies to Tampa tomorrow." I shrug. "It's kind of nice to get caught up in it all. The past year has been hell for me and this all seems like a too-good-to-be-true dream."

"But you're okay with it?" Claire asks, her blue eyes assessing as they search mine. "Because I know you feel like you have to do this but you really don't."

Indy wrings her hands. "Claire and I were talking and—"

I shake my head, cutting her off. "I love you both, very much, for looking out for me the way you have. It means more to me than you will ever know just that you would offer to bail me out financially. But I've seen more friendships and relationships ruined by money than anything else."

Indy frowns. She knows very little about my family, and

Claire, only a tiny bit more. But there once was a time when Dad and Jerry Jensen were like brothers, their relationship thicker than blood. Until a deal went wrong, fortunes were lost, and their friendship was destroyed. I didn't know any of these details when I accepted Jerry's offer to help me with college. Up until that point, he'd been like an uncle to me. Sure, things seemed a little strained when Dad and Jerry were in the same room but I figured it was because of a stressful deal they were working on. Not because they carried blame and contempt for each other. Once I accepted the loan, Jerry hiked up the interest rate to ensure a Carter would be forever in his debt. In a way, he burned my last bridge home. But today is my wedding day and there's no room for Dad or Jerry in my thoughts.

"I made a deal with Torsten, and I'm going to stick to it. Besides"—I give a little twirl, my dress flaring perfectly—"if this is how it's kicking off, with all this glamour and perfection, it's going to be great, right?"

Indy nods enthusiastically. Her brown hair is swept to the side in a complicated braid that hangs over her left shoulder. She's got stars in her eyes, a common occurrence since she fell in love with Noah Scotch. Claire regards me a little more realistically but after a moment, she smiles. "I hope so, Ri. You ready to go?"

I nod, turning to cast one last look at myself in the mirror. I'm ready.

OUR CITY HALL service takes a grand total of seven minutes. Claire was right, we garnered *a lot* of attention.

With the three of us girls done up like we're headed to the Emmys and the guys all hulking and dangerously handsome in their suits and sports coats, even the judge raises her eyebrows when Torsten and I are called up. The process is easy and efficient. Given the magnitude of the decision, the legal implications, the significance of it all, I thought it would take longer.

Instead, we recite a few words, sign our names, and smile for the flash of a camera. Then, Torsten kisses me deeply in front of the entire room. I giggle, he grins, and then sweeps the group, all nine of us, to The Ivy for a celebratory lunch.

"Damn, he's pulling out the big guns," Claire murmurs to me as we enter The Ivy. It's a swanky, downtown restaurant renowned for its creative menu and world-class mixologists. I used to think getting a reservation was nearly impossible, but since learning the ease with which Noah Scotch manages to obtain them, I'm beginning to rethink that assumption.

Today, we're led to a private room in the back. When I step inside, my breath catches in my throat.

"Wow," Claire breathes out.

"Stunning," Indy agrees, stopping beside me.

The three of us look up, to where hundreds of flower petals hang on nearly invisible threads from the ceiling, down the entire length of the table. It gives the illusion that petals are being sprinkled from the heavens, floating gently to Earth at different speeds. Three big centerpieces with white roses, blue hydrangeas, and baby's breath, dot the table, surrounded by tiny flickering tea lights.

The table is set for nine, with printed menus and name tags resting on each plate. Champagne flutes are already poured, waiting for a toast.

"Do you like it?" Torsten asks. His hand skates down my back, his fingertips brushing against my spine.

I shiver from his touch, my body going both hot and cold at his proximity. Just two nights ago, those fingers, that mouth, made me come undone. And now, Torsten is my husband, giving me a fairy tale wedding day that people dream about.

None of this is real, I remind myself. I *need* to remind myself.

Because when I turn around and fall into the shimmering, bottomless, blue pools of Torsten's eyes, it sure as hell doesn't seem fake. Not the worry in the tightness of his lips, not the hint of hope in the rings around his irises, and definitely not in his possessive touch as his arm wraps around my waist.

"It's beautiful," I tell him the truth. He smiles and it's mesmerizing, hitting me straight in the chest.

How the hell did this beautiful man go this long without a serious female attachment in his life? Why did he choose me? Any woman would have leapt at the chance, with zero conditions, to be standing where I am right now, in his arms, under a freaking blanket of petals. Why would he ask me and voluntarily go half a million dollars into debt?

"You're beautiful, Ri," he murmurs, surprising the hell out of me when he leans forward and brushes a kiss over my lips. "Happy wedding day, sweetheart."

My lips tingle and a jolt of desire shoots through me. I practically melt into Torsten, wanting more, wanting him. My head feels fuzzy, the room suddenly hazy. He grins, tips my chin up, and kisses me again. This time it's long and deep, soulful and sensual. I grip his shoulders and press my breasts into his chest. It feels like I'm drowning and gulping oxygen at the same time.

The cheers and whistles of our friends ring out around us and I have the sudden urge to smile.

The flash of a camera way too close to my face pops and I pull back, dazed. Torsten swipes the pad of his thumb over his bottom lip, as if to wipe away my lipstick, before turning to have a few words with the photographer.

I feel lightheaded and unsteady on my feet. That kiss was all-consuming. It was intense and passionate and all. for.

show. Of course Torsten hired a photographer; I saw him and his camera at City Hall. It's all part of the act, all part of making this look real.

By the happy smiles of our friends, even the ones who don't know the full story, Torsten and I are pulling it off. I should feel relieved. Not hollow. Or hurt.

Claire sets a glass of champagne in my hand and gives me a worried glance.

I take a sip, savor the taste. It tastes expensive, one of the finer things in life I haven't had in a long time.

"You okay?" Claire whispers.

I nod, taking another sip. My gaze flits to our friend group, laughing and talking. Everyone has a drink in hand. The atmosphere is jovial; it *feels* like a true celebration.

"That looked intense," she adds.

"Felt intense," I admit.

Claire's hand wraps around my wrist and I look at my best friend.

"You sure you know what you're doing, Ri?"

I shake my head, keeping a small smile on my face in case anyone, such as the photographer, looks over. "Not a goddamn clue."

Claire squeezes my hand and I smile for the camera.

Flash.

IT'S NOT LATE when we get home, barely 7 p.m. But it feels as if I've lived a hundred days today and the fatigue of it all—the marriage, the celebration, the champagne—hits me hard. My eyelids are half closed by the time I step into the penthouse.

A week ago, I was fighting off Stu's wandering hands, wondering what life in an alleyway would look like.

Now, I'm stepping out of shoes that cost almost as much as my old car in a luxury penthouse. Talk about a twist of fate.

On some level, I know it should bother me that I'm doing something highly illegal. I'm sure I should have some moral qualms about the whole arrangement. Maybe the past year, of trying so damn hard to just survive, has warped my thinking. Because right now, I'm so happy to be full and warm and safe, I could weep tears of joy.

"You have fun today?" Torsten asks. His voice is all rumbly and deep.

God, he's sexy. His blue eyes blaze as he unbuttons the neat row of his dress shirt. I watch as he undoes his cuff links. They're shiny and look heavy, expensive. Like him.

What does he think when he looks at me?

Torsten tilts his head, studying me. "You okay, Ri?"

I nod. Torsten Hansen is now my husband. *Husband.* My heartbeat races at the thought. I'm falling a little bit in like and lust for my husband. But not in love, right? No, never in love.

The weight of an important decision settles around my neck. In many ways, it seems heavier than the decision over whether or not to marry Torsten in the first place.

"If we sleep together..." I say and Torsten's eyebrows jump to his hairline. I clear my throat. "If we sleep together, it will complicate things."

He nods slowly.

"But if we don't, we'll just be celibate for two years..."

He nods again, frowning. He takes a step closer and his big hand envelops mine. It's warm and strong, reassuring and tempting.

I lick my lips and Torsten's eyes focus on my mouth. He swallows, his Adam's apple bobbing up and down. "Rielle."

"If we do this, it's just about sex. We both have physical

needs; there's no point in going without for two years when we're here, right?"

He frowns, his eyes flashing with a burst of anger. He shuffles closer, his hand squeezing mine.

"No messy emotions, no complicated expectations. It's easy to get carried away after a day like today." I force a smile and unzip the back of my dress. I shimmy out of the top and push it down to my waist. It falls to the floor like a waterfall, rippling and rushing down my body.

Torsten takes a step back, his eyes scanning my curves. He closes his eyes for a moment, as if in pain. "Rielle, we could try—"

"No," I cut him off. I don't want to hear whatever he's going to say. Because any words from him right now will make me yearn for the fairy tale that doesn't exist. He'll make me crave the happily-ever-after that isn't in the cards for us.

I know better than to hope for things like that.

I step out of my dress, my hands dangling at my sides. I force myself to say the words I need to believe. "Tonight, going forward, this"—I gesture between us—"is just sex."

His eyes are narrowed as they study my face. After a moment, he nods. "Just sex." His tone is clipped.

I swallow and step forward, my hands finding his shoulders, my body pressing into his. I kiss him hard, hunger and hurt on my lips. His hands find my hips and squeeze. He meets me kiss for kiss, our teeth clashing, our tongues dueling.

Torsten Hansen fucks me fast and furious on his living room floor hours after he kissed me under a sky of rose petals. He takes me like a savage and I revel in it, in him. Afterwards, when we're both sated, he storms to his bathroom to clean up and I retreat to my bedroom so I don't have to witness the hurt and confusion in his eyes.

It's for the best if we stick to the arrangement. Today was beautiful; it was more than perfect. But it was also dangerous and I need to remember that. My heart can't handle any more breaks. At least, these are the rationalizations I feed myself as I toss and turn all night. Around 3 a.m., I finally fall asleep.

When I wake in the morning and step into the kitchen, Torsten's gone. He's already left for his flight. A simple note is tucked under a coffee mug on the island.

Ri, Be back in three days. Here's a card for whatever you need. Torsten.

A lump squeezes my throat painfully. I pick up the gold credit card, threading it through my fingers.

"Dammit." I toss it back on the island. Tears rush to the surface and a few of them spill over, tracking down my cheeks.

If I'm keeping things casual, then why the hell does this sting so badly? Yesterday morning, I felt cherished and desired.

Today, I just feel cheap.

What's worse? I deserve it.

"I can't believe you got married yesterday," Claire mutters as she drives to my old apartment, where Sally is parked. I still owe several months of rent and need to move out the rest of my things. Torsten promised to help me sort it all out when he gets back from Tampa but after everything that went down between us, I don't want to become overly dependent on him.

I didn't touch the gold credit card he left me.

Torsten is taking care of my Jerry Jensen loan. It doesn't feel right to let him settle my three months of overdue rent and haul my boxes to his penthouse. I'm the one who pushed him to adhere to the terms we agreed to. I made my bed and now I need to lie in it. Even if it fucking sucks.

"Yeah," I agree, looking out the window.

"Ri? What's going on?" Claire asks, turning into the parking lot of my apartment building. She parks and turns off Easton's car.

I drop my head back against the headrest, rolling it to meet her expectant expression.

"Before the wedding, Torsten and I..." I pause, weighing my words.

"You slept with him, didn't you?" she deadpans, not looking remotely surprised.

"No! I mean, we did *stuff.*"

Claire snorts. "Stuff? What are you, fourteen?"

I feel the blush work up my cheeks and Claire's mouth drops open. She points at me. "You really like him, Ri, don't you?"

I squeeze my eyes closed. "I can't like him, Claire. I mean, I can't like him more than just a friend. We made an arrangement; we signed a contract."

"So?" She shrugs. "Things change."

"When we did…stuff—"

She sighs.

"It was intense. Real." I widen my eyes at her.

"Okay." She widens her eyes back.

"Then our wedding was so much more than I thought it would be."

"It was pretty magical," Claire agrees. "A hell of a lot nicer than most real weddings."

"I know. It messed with my head. I can't tell what's real and what's not. The room was decorated so beautifully and then Torsten kissed me and I was freaking melting like one of those girls."

"What girls?"

I glare at her. "Like Indy. Or you."

She snickers.

"And then, the freaking flash of the camera went off and Torsten gives me this knowing look, like 'Hey, we're killing the documentation for our papers.'"

Claire winces.

"Sometimes, he looks at me like he cares about me more than anything in the world and other times, his words make it seem like this is all about the arrangement. It's confusing and I don't like feeling like this."

"Like what?" Claire shifts in her seat, giving me her full attention, her expression serious.

"Like I don't know which way is up. It's unnerving and frustrating. And frankly, I'm not good at it."

Claire nods. "You like to be in control."

"I *am* in control."

"Okay." She holds her hands up in surrender.

I roll my eyes. "Which is why last night, I told Torsten we need to stick to the agreement. But it's stupid that we're going to both forgo sex for two damn years, right? I mean, people have needs. And it's not like I'm *not* attracted to him. So…"

"You had sex on your wedding night?"

I bite my bottom lip and nod.

"And?" she prompts.

"It was incredible in terms of our chemistry. But everything else," I sigh, exasperated, "it didn't feel anything like it did when we just did *stuff*."

Claire winces. "Ri, I have no idea how you're holding everything together right now. The past week, your entire life has been flipped upside down. Everything you've been working your ass off for has disappeared career wise and you're married to a guy you barely know but it's obvious, you want to *get to know*."

I snort.

"Cut yourself some slack," Claire advises. "You and Torsten will sort things out but take it from someone who's been in weird, relationship-y limbo, honesty really is the best policy."

"I guess."

"You guess?"

I shrug. "I'm overwhelmed."

"Fair."

"I'm fine with our agreement. I need to find a job and Torsten needs to focus on the playoffs."

"Okay." Claire drags the word out, trying to figure out where I'm going with this.

"But I can't just give up all my control and let him take care of my life, of me. We're not just moving my boxes today. I'm going to sell Sally, pay off the rent money I owe, and hustle for a job. He left me a freaking credit card and it just made me feel so…"

"So…what?"

"Needy," I supply.

Claire rolls her eyes and huffs. "You're really overthinking this. Torsten left you a credit card because part of your agreement is that he looks after the finances. You don't have to sell Sally, reacquaint yourself with public transportation, and pinch pennies because you're too proud to take what he's offering."

When she puts it like that, I sound like an overindulgent child, throwing a tantrum. Still, using my own money fills me with a sense of security that I crave. Claire won't understand the depth of it because I've never let her in enough to truly understand. Instead of explaining, I shrug. "I'm doing it anyway."

She rolls her eyes but doesn't look surprised. Living together for four years has proved that when I make my mind up about something, there's very little that will alter my decision. "Who's buying your car?"

I glance out the windshield and tip my chin up when I spot Merck. "Merck's hooking me up with an interested party."

"Oh, brother," Claire grumbles, but she follows me out of the car.

"Hey, Rielle," Merck greets me, his neck tattoo stretching when he cranes his neck to get a look at Claire. "What's up?" he says to her, sliding his baseball hat off of his head, turning it around, and placing it back down so it's backwards.

"Hey," she says. Then she turns to me and holds out her

hand. "Give me your keys. It's a relief you rented a furnished apartment and we don't have to carry a couch down the stairs. I'll start boxing up your things."

"You don't have to—"

She sticks her tongue out at me and I snicker, placing my keys in her palm.

Merck and I watch Claire in silence until she steps through the door of my apartment building.

"You still owe three months of rent," Merck reminds me in his thick Southie accent. The cool April sunlight gleams off the hard planes of his face as he turns his head to gesture for a green van to exit the parking lot.

"I know. I'm going to settle up with you today."

Merck looks heavenward, as if asking God for patience. He's a little bit scary and does a shitty job maintaining the apartment building but he's always been *fair*. "You really want to sell your car?"

I nod.

"Rielle, I don't know what the hell you did to end up here."

"What—"

He shakes his head and my words die on my tongue. Merck waves a hand in my direction. "Girl, you and I both know you didn't grow up in parts like these."

I bite my bottom lip. He has me there. I grew up in an 8,000 square foot home with a closet larger than my apartment. I grew up donning the hottest trends, flying private, and looking down at the world from penthouses in cities around the world. I grew up with a mother who made me feel like I could do anything I set my mind to and a father who made me feel like I couldn't.

"I see you hustling. I know you're on your grind. But girl, really, you're not cut out for this life and I'm not trying to be a dick when I say I'm glad to see you go. You call Daddy and apologize for whatever the fuck went down?"

"Nah, I finally reached out to my friends for support."

"Good call. There's an expiration date on living like this." He swings his arm wide to encompass the dilapidated apartment buildings, the cracked asphalt with weeds that look like mini forests sprouting up, and the trash that litters the space. "You stay too long, it gets under your skin. If it gets too deep, you can't get rid of it. It's a stench that follows you everywhere. It's not just a period in your twenties but your whole fucking life." He raises his eyebrows at me.

I bend mine back. "How do you know that?"

He snorts and pulls a cigarette pack from his back pocket. He taps the end of the pack against his palm a few times before pulling one out and slipping it between his lips. He offers me one. I shake my head and his grin grows. "I didn't grow up like this either, girl. But I didn't heed the warnings when I got 'em either. I didn't reach out for the support like I should've. Like you are. But I always knew you were smarter than me."

"It's not too late for you, Merck."

He chuckles, his eyes scanning the parking lot before piercing mine. "Yeah, it is."

A car pulls into the lot and Merck raises a hand over his eyebrows, squinting against the sunlight. "That's Rick. Whatever you get for your car, we'll call your rent paid in full."

I jerk back by the offer. We both know Sally isn't going to fetch three months of overdue rent. Rielle from last week would have insisted on paying back every single cent. Rielle today is taking degrees of help when it's offered and doing her best to be okay with it. "Thank you, Merck."

"Better not see you back here, girl."

I glance at my old apartment door. "You won't," I promise.

An hour later, I wave goodbye to Sally. As her burned-out taillights bump out of the parking lot, I breathe out a shaky exhale. I got two grand for her. Right now, I need to be grateful for that and not upset that I no longer have a ride anywhere.

I steel my shoulders, smack the envelope with cash against my palm, and head to Merck's office.

"That was fast." He grins when he sees me.

I pass him the envelope. "It's two thousand."

He peers inside the envelope and nods. "Take care of yourself, Ri."

"That's it?" I shuffle from one foot to the next, waiting for the fine print I missed last time.

But Merck proves to be a much more considerate person than Jerry Jensen. "That's it. Have a nice life."

I snort. "You too. And Merck?"

He slips an unlit cigarette between his lips and leans back in his chair, waiting.

"Thank you," I say sincerely.

He snorts and waves me away but I see the color that heightens in his cheeks.

I laugh and make my way back to my apartment.

When I enter, Claire is rolling my old suitcase to the door. "Hey. How'd it go?"

"Sally is gone."

She wrinkles her nose. "I'm sorry, Ri. I know you loved her."

"She was my ride or die," I admit.

Claire flips me the middle finger before gesturing to the boxes she packed up. "I'm your ride or die, bitch."

I laugh and toss an arm around her shoulder. "Yeah, you are. Thanks for doing this."

"You're welcome. So, you're all settled with rent?"

I nod.

"Good. I sorted through your clothes." Claire points out several bags. "One is for donate, one is for sell, one you need to go through. But some of these designer pieces could fetch some good money." She shakes her head at me. "If you're set on not touching Torsten's credit card, or accepting any of my *help*—"

I wrinkle my nose in objection.

Claire rolls her eyes. "Then you're going to need some cash to hold you over until you find a new job."

I nod, knowing she's right. "That's genius, Claire. I don't know why I didn't sell my clothes earlier." Thanks to my affluent upbringing and the suitcases packed with clothes I snuck out of my dad's home the night I ran away to college, I always looked better than I lived. Even though I scraped and scrimped for the past year, I also learned how to wear the same basic staples and accessorize smartly to give the appearance of having more than I do.

Now, my clothes are coming in handy in a different way.

"Stop." Claire holds up her hand. "I can't handle thinking of how you lived over the past year and never told me. Or worse, how I didn't realize it." She turns her big blue eyes on mine. "I'm sorry, Ri. I was so caught up in my own drama, in not having a job, in getting swept up with East...I've been a shitty friend."

I hold my arms wide to encompass all the boxes and bags she sorted through and packed up. "Stop. You're my best friend. I'm sorry I wasn't honest with you."

She gives me a big hug and squeezes too tightly.

"I'm really fucking hungry," she says as her stomach grumbles. "So I need you to accept my invitation to lunch because I don't want to eat alone and I don't want to waste time having one of those dumb back-and-forth conversations where we argue over who is going to pay the bill."

I laugh. "Deal. I happily accept your invite. I'm hungry too."

Claire rolls her eyes. "I don't know how you worked up an appetite. All you had to do was stand in a parking lot and talk to a couple of guys with sick ink while I slaved away up here, doing manual labor."

I snicker and pick up a box. "Shut it. We'll load up the car and go eat."

"The Mexican fusion restaurant I'm obsessed with?" she asks hopefully.

"Whatever you want, Claire," I agree. "Thanks for today."

"Duh. As if you'd piss off your new husband with anyone *but* me."

We both laugh as we carry my few boxes down to her car. As we pull out of the parking lot, I glance at the building one last time in Easton's car's side mirror. Relief rolls through me as it grows smaller. I'm happy to be putting it behind me, just like Merck said.

CHAPTER TEN
TORSTEN

My thumb runs along the length of my wedding band.

What the hell was I thinking?

After a flight to sunny Florida, a skate to help clear my head, and some good-natured ribbing by my teammates, I should be over it.

Rielle and I made a deal. We signed a contract.

It shouldn't bother me that I stroked and coaxed her body into the sweetest submission one night and fucked her hard and dirty the next. I should be happy that our sexual connection, our chemistry, is off the goddamn charts.

Instead, I'm pissed off; that one night she looked at me like a man she trusts, like a man she could give her heart to, and the next, like a stranger who can get her off quickly.

What the hell changed in the time between kissing her rosebud mouth at the altar and being on the receiving end of her glare on our wedding night? Does she regret getting married? Did she finally wake up and realize all that she's sacrificing by making this commitment? The years in her twenties that she could be out, dating, settling down with a man who truly owns her soul, making babies?

Fuck. I spring from the desk chair in my hotel room, restless energy coursing through my body like electricity. There's nowhere for it to go so it keeps building, layer upon layer, until I feel ready to combust. My hands clench into fists and I check the time again.

I have another hour to kill before I can head to the arena. I'm desperate to get on the ice and play tonight. The game, the mental focus it requires, the physical release it encourages, I'm ready to lose myself in it completely.

A knock at the door has me striding toward it and pulling it wide open.

I grin when I see it's James Ryan, the other Hawks defenseman. More than anything, I wish I had confided in him about my sham of a marriage. I know Rielle and I desperately needed to limit the number of people who knew the truth but James would have been a solid guy to reach out to for advice.

"Hey," I say, holding the door open wider. "What's going on?"

James squints at me, his expression grave, his eyes searching. "You tell me. You in some type of trouble?"

I chuckle and shake my head. "Why would you think that?"

James gives me a look and pushes past me into my hotel room. "You got married out of the blue to a girl no one knew you were even dating. You're broody—"

I blanch. I don't brood. Glower, maybe. But broody?

"You're quieter than normal too." James points at me accusingly.

I shrug. "Just got a lot going on right now."

"Torst, my life is a mess. It's been one big fucking disaster for the past year. For me to even notice that you're checked out means you're more than checked out. So, what's going on?"

I wince at the bluntness with which he says the words. A little over a year ago, James's wife passed from cancer, leaving him and their young twins behind. He's been grappling with her loss ever since, existing on autopilot. He shows up when and where he's supposed to. He volunteers for field trips and waits in school pickup lines. He signs autographs when someone asks him to. But I haven't seen him really smile since Layla died. I'm not sure if he knows how to anymore.

"I know you're hurting, man. And I'm sorry."

James runs a hand over three-day-old stubble. His gray eyes flash, angry and anguished. "I'm not hurting, Torsten. I'm not anything except numb."

I don't believe him for a second but empathy rocks through me at his tortured expression. James and I came up through the ranks together. We've been the starting defensive line for years and a cornerstone of the Hawks team. He's only a few years younger than me and yet, he's lived what seems like a hundred years more.

"I have no idea what you're going through, Ryan, but if there's anything I can do to help…"

He shakes his head. "Appreciate it, man. But I'm not so easily distracted by deflection anymore. Tell me what's going on with you."

I grapple with how much truth to share with James. For years, I was the guy with his heart on his sleeve, an open book, a call-it-like-I-see-it kind of man. Now, it's as if everyone gets varying degrees of the truth, just shades of my honesty. It leaves me feeling rotten, like less of the principled guy I held myself up to be for years. I guess marrying not for love is a gateway for other, less desirable traits. I blow out a breath. "Man, I can't tell you everything."

He frowns. "You in trouble?"

I shake my head. "You're a steel vault, right?" I meet his eye and after a second, he nods. I trust all the guys on my team, some more than others. But James is up there. "My knee never fully recovered from my last surgery. My shoulder is fucked up."

James frowns at me, sitting down in the desk chair. He leans forward until his elbows rest on his knees. "What are you talking about?"

I grab two bottles of water from the mini-fridge and toss one to him. I place mine down so I can rest my left hand over the right side of my chest. Slowly, I rotate my shoulder. The loud popping and clicking sounds ring out in the quiet space and James winces.

"Physio? Treatments?"

"I've pretty much run the gamut. Look, I'm going to be thirty-eight. I'm getting too old for this and I know it. I'm not re-signing."

James sits straight up in his chair, his eyes narrowed, his expression grim. After a moment, he scrapes his hand over his face. "Fuck."

"I need to be realistic."

"You had an incredible career."

"It wasn't awful," I agree.

He gives me a lopsided smile, understanding and compassion in his eyes. No one wants to see a player go. When you do, it makes you start counting down how much time you have left. But for a guy like James, whose been through hell this year, playing hockey doesn't hold the same weight it once did. "What does this have to do with marriage?"

I shrug. "It's time, James. I need to start thinking about the next chapter of my life."

"Okay. But this girl, Rielle—"

"She's a good woman."

"How well do you really know her?"

"Enough to know I could spend the rest of my life by her side and be happy." Once the words are out, I realize the truth behind them. Rielle could make me happy forever; it's me who can never make her light up like the sun.

James gives me a long, searching look. After a moment, he

sighs, and I know that he knows there's more to this than I'm willing to discuss. "Then why the long face?"

"It's complicated."

He chuckles and it's the first time I've heard him almost-laugh in months that I look up, surprised. He shakes his head at me. "What do you need, Torst?"

"Well, now that you're here, I'm not opposed to a little advice. You're right, things with Ri happened fast. We don't really *know* each other the way most couples do when they marry. But I know the parts that matter to me the most. I know the kind of woman she is."

"And that's great, man. But Torsten, marriage isn't just some agreement you make for a few years. It's a lifelong commitment. It's sacred and special. You say *vows*."

I swallow against the tightness in my throat. Heat spreads across the back of my neck. James would feel sorry for me if he knew that I said *vows* knowing I was going to break them. But God, I don't want to. I'm desperate for even a shred of what James shared with Layla. I just have no clue how the hell to create that with a woman who has her whole life ahead of her, one who married me for all the wrong reasons.

Do Ri and I even stand a chance? Getting married for a green card and a loan buyout is clearly starting off on the wrong foot.

I uncap my water bottle and take a long swig. When I slam it back down on the dresser, James swears.

I look up and freeze. Because James, my old friend, is looking at me in pure disbelief.

"What?" I ask.

"Jesus, Torsten. You want this for real, don't you? I thought it was some kind of midlife crisis. Some desperate attempt to fill some void, to deal with the weight of almost turning forty. But you want the whole thing, the vows and the marriage and the *wife*."

Pins and needles travel up and down my limbs at the

truth, the *accusation*, in James's tone. I feel exposed in a way I never have before but after years of being on my own, with no one to count on or trust save for Farmor nearly 3,500 miles away, yeah, I fucking want it.

James leans back in his chair and rolls the water bottle between his hands. "Never thought I'd see the day."

"What day?"

"The day that Torsten Hansen truly wanted something more than one night only. Or, in this case, one month only."

"Rielle is my wife, James."

He nods, considering my words. "Do you trust her?"

"Yes."

"Does she care about your best interests?"

"Yeah."

"Is it all about the money or social status?"

I chuckle, remembering how Rielle wanted to pay half my rent. I never bothered to tell her I own the penthouse outright. There's not even a mortgage. "Not at all."

"Do you guys laugh when nothing's funny? Do you enjoy her company?" He lifts an eyebrow at me.

Slowly, I nod.

He smiles back. "Then there's hope for you yet. You don't have to be madly, passionately in love, although that helps." He tilts his head toward mine, his eyes serious. "You need to have the foundation of a friendship, the ability to communicate, and the desire to care. If you're starting off with that, you may be able to grow a relationship that blossoms into the kind of love you're searching for."

I stare at him for a long moment, suddenly realizing just how much he, Milly, and Mason truly lost when Layla passed. "I don't know if I'll ever have even half of what you did with Layla. But fuck, James, I'm so sorry you lost her."

He dips his head and a long beat passes. When he meets my eyes again, his are ringed in a sadness so acute, I feel it in my chest. "I hope you do, Torsten. As for me, I'm just grateful as fuck I got to have Layla for as long as I did."

I nod, a lump of emotion swelling in my chest.

James stands from his chair. "Come on." He clasps my shoulder. "We've got a game to win. Everything you're twisted up over, and trust me, you're going to have more days feeling like this, put it into your play. Turn off the thoughts eating at you, and channel everything you're messed up over into your performance tonight. At least then, you'll go to bed feeling better about something."

I snicker, seeing the merit in his advice. I shoulder my bag and follow James out of the hotel room. As I wait for him to grab his stuff before we head to the lobby to meet the team, it strikes me that this is one of the last times I'll be doing this.

Hanging with all the guys, gearing up for a game, trying to mentally all get in the same headspace. For years, my team has been my family. Now, I'm desperate to create one with Rielle. And it fucking hurts to know that on top of losing hockey, I'll never have with her what I truly want most. Even if James believes otherwise.

I GLIDE DOWN THE ICE, the cold air rushing by. With a stick in hand, ice beneath my skates, and a packed arena, I feel settled for the first time since I married Rielle.

Some of the anxiety I've been holding in my chest recedes as I lock into the game, my body tensing for the second period face-off. Tampa gains possession of the puck and I angle my body in between the puck carrier and the net, skating backwards until we're battling it out in the corner.

"Come on, old man," number seventy-two mutters, his

shoulder slamming into mine. Kid's been trash talking all night, trying to get me off my game. A few seasons ago, it might have worked. But right now, I keep my focus on the puck.

The hit vibrates down my arm, like pins and needles. I hear his loud breathing and his obnoxious chuckle but I don't pay him any mind. We keep at it in the corner until I gain control of the puck and initiate a clean breakout, skating furiously until I can flip the puck to Easton.

Seventy-two flies by me and I shake my head.

The rest of the period passes in a blur. I give everything I have to the game, leave everything on the ice. Knowing this is my last season, my last time in the playoffs, maybe even my last game fuels my determination to make every play one of my best.

We win 5–3 and the team breathes a collective sigh of relief. We're up two to one and need best of seven to advance to the second round. "Good game." Austin grasps my shoulder and squeezes.

My shoulder screams in protest after taking two hard hits in the third period. I wince, Austin frowns, but I laugh it off. This is my last season and I'm going to see it through.

After a quick team meeting, we all go our separate ways with plans to meet up later for a drink at the hotel bar. Back in my hotel room, I debate whether or not to call Rielle.

Does she want to hear from me? Did she watch the game? Will she even pick up?

My stomach twists and I feel more freaking nervous about calling my wife than I did playing tonight. I snort at myself. *Man up, Hansen. You married this woman; you want a future with her. The least you can do is call her, check in, make sure she's okay after you took off with the morning light and no goodbye.*

Working a swallow, I pick up my phone, pleased to see that she texted me.

RIELLE

Great game! Congrats on the win!

I can't stop the goofy grin that splits my face. I tap Rielle's name.

It rings twice and then, "Torsten."

I smile. "Hey, Ri."

"Hey," I say, some of the knots that have been twisted in my stomach since I woke up to Torsten's note, loosening.

"You watched the game."

"You were amazing," I tell him the truth. "I wanted to knock that punk out," I add, impressed that he never lost his cool with the dick who spent more time goading him than controlling the puck.

He chuckles and the sound warms my chest.

I lean back into the couch cushions of his living room, tucking my feet up beneath me. The lights of the city twinkle below but up here, in Torsten's penthouse, I feel a million miles away. In fact, for a brief instant, before he called, I felt like I did at my dad's house since Mom passed. Apart, separate, lonely.

"How are you feeling?" I ask, knowing that the few hits he took must have taken their toll.

He blows out a breath. "I'm okay. It's easier to wrap my head around it all knowing my time on the ice is almost up."

Melancholy mixed with acceptance wraps around his words and I bite my bottom lip, unsure what to say next. Is he a little relieved this is his last season? Is he bitter? Is he both and doesn't know which emotion should win out?

"What'd you do today?" he asks, pulling my thoughts back to the conversation.

I worry my lip between my teeth, debating if I should tell him the truth. But honesty was part of *our* vows, not the ones we said in the courtroom, but the ones we agreed to beforehand. "I saw your credit card."

"I don't want you to feel bad about it. It's part of our agreement and—"

"I sold my car," I blurt out.

"What? Why?" I hear him shift through the line, maybe sitting straight up. "Today?"

"Yeah, Claire came with me. I—look Torsten, I feel really shitty about our wedding night."

"Ri, sweetheart, I'm sorry I—"

"It's my fault," I cut him off again. "I don't know how to do this with you. I know what we agreed to but sometimes when we're together, things get...*blurred*. Confusing."

"It's complicated," he agrees. "Tell me what you want, Ri. Don't even think about it, just say whatever you're feeling."

I twist my hair around my finger, tugging on it as emotions I'm unprepared to deal with rise to the surface. "I'm fine with our arrangement, really. And I wanted things to happen between us the other night. It's just that, it's confusing what's real and what's not. I don't want to rely on you so much, to need you for anything. It will just be harder when our agreement ends."

"I'd never not be here for you, Rielle."

"I haven't let anyone in in a really long time, Torst. Trust and full transparency are new for me. Needing someone, relying on another person, it's really hard for me to give up any control over my life. I don't want to need your money. I don't want your credit card. The fact that I'm living in your place, in a freaking penthouse, when last week, I was going to be homeless, it's messing with my head. And then, when we...sleep together, it makes me feel...cheap. Like I'm completely selling myself short, taking the easy way out, and using my body to exist."

He's quiet for a long moment and I worry I've somehow offended him. But when he speaks, his voice is raw, as if he's hurting for me more than himself. "Fuck, Ri. I never want to make you, make any woman, feel that way. I—shit, babe, you know it's not like that, right? I'd do anything I can to make your life easier, better, regardless if you never even hug me again."

I snort, my emotions clogging my throat at the sincerity in his tone.

"I know. It's just that I don't know how to trust it yet. Does that make sense? It's not you, Torst, it's—"

"It's not you either, sweetheart. It's the situations you've been in."

"Maybe," I say, even though it is me. I'm defective when it comes to relationships and love. If I wasn't, wouldn't Dad or my brother, Jesse, have reached out by now? Wouldn't any of my childhood playmates, Jerry Jensen's son Dennis, have contacted me?

"So, you sold your car?" he prods.

"I did. I settled up my rent."

He swears. "You're not going to use the card, are you?"

"No."

He snorts. "Do me a favor? Put it in your wallet anyway."

"I—"

"I don't care if you use it or not. Just keep it with you in case you ever need it, okay? Give me some peace of mind here, Ri. My God, you are stubborn."

I chuckle, relieved he's not fighting me on this. Maybe it's because he doesn't really care. But deep down, I think it's because he knows he won't win.

"You okay at the apartment by yourself?" he asks.

"Yeah, I'm good. When do you come home?"

"Why?" he asks slyly. "You planning on being gone or you missing me that much?"

I grin at his teasing tone but if I listen carefully, I detect the uncertainty buried underneath his words. Knowing he's holding back a lot of his thoughts to make me feel more comfortable, more in control of this situation, I tell him the truth. "I'm looking forward to spending time together."

He laughs again, louder this time. "Me too, sweetheart. I'm back in two days. Let me take you for brunch? Or dinner? Whatever you want. Just let me take you someplace nice."

"Show me off?" I guess, knowing we need to make some appearances together.

"Be with you," he amends and I grin in spite of myself. "I want to talk to you about this summer. About Oslo."

"You really want me to meet your family?" I ask hesitantly, the knots in my stomach tugging tightly. Pulling off our sham of a marriage for practical purposes is one thing, lying to his family's faces is another.

"No," he says and it pierces my chest. "I just want to fulfill my grandmother's wishes. She wants you to come."

"Oh, okay." I stammer, "Well, um, can I think about it?"

"Of course. Listen, Ri, I've gotta meet the guys for a celebratory drink."

"Right. I'll talk you later."

"I'm glad you messaged."

"Yeah. Thanks for calling." I disconnect the call, feeling more out of sorts than before Torsten and I spoke.

I can't figure anything out with Torsten. I have no idea where I stand with him. I told him that sleeping together is too confusing and he readily agreed. He wants to bring me to Oslo but doesn't really want me to meet his family. I thought that speaking with him would clear up some of the uncertainty I feel about how to proceed with our marriage.

Instead, I'm left with more conflicting feelings. More questions I don't have the answers to.

Did he want to have sex with me because we agreed not to have sex with other people? Or did he really desire *me*? Is he fine having a chill, friendship type of marriage? But then, why bring me across the Atlantic Ocean and prop me up to his frail grandmother as so much more than that?

I sigh and stand from the couch. I walk the perimeter of the penthouse, glancing down at Boston. The old and the new, the historical and the modern. It's a beautiful city and I'm happy that out of all the places in the world I could have landed, I made it here.

It's still early so I brew a cup of tea and open my laptop. Feeling a little nostalgic, I open the files I've kept of my college work, my eye catching on the folder titled "photography." When I open it, a myriad of images loads on my screen and I lean closer, studying the photos I shot for various assignments.

I enjoyed it more than I ever admitted. I liked being on the other side of the lens, the person capturing the emotions instead of having them ripple across *my* face, for all to see. There was a secrecy to it, a safety I reveled in. I took photography courses all through university and as I scroll through the folder, I note where my skill level improved, where I began experimenting more, where my passion just started to peak through.

But then I graduated, landed a role at Hendrix, and lost myself for nearly a year.

I click on a search engine and check out some photography studios in Boston, my eyes nearly falling out of my head at the price of courses, not to mention the cost of a camera. A quick flash of Torsten's credit card whips through my mind but I shut that idea down.

Marrying Torsten is a fresh start. It's a chance to get back on my feet, to move forward with my life. It's not an opportunity to find myself at his expense. It's not an invitation to take advantage of his generosity. Or twist his friendship into a relationship that will never last, that will leave us both hurting.

I just need to remember that.

"Hey Bill," I answer the phone, pressing my finger into my ear so I can hear him better. "We're just about to take off." The team's already on the plane and we're all a little desperate to head back to Boston with another win under our belts. Our second game was a tough loss but we're still leading the series 3-2.

"Hi, Torsten. Oh, okay. This will only take a second then. I know where you stand regarding next season but since you haven't formally put out a public statement yet, you're still getting endorsement offers. Autumn just called me"—he mentions my agent who I really need to check in with—"about a vodka deal. The marketing company is making a big push for athletic endorsements, and you're at the top of their list."

"What's the brand?" I ask, grinning my thanks to the stewardess who places a tea in my hand.

"Saint."

"Never heard of it." I blow on the hot tea.

"They're relatively new. They're working with Hendrix Marketing and since it's a Boston-based—"

"Hendrix?" I clarify. It can't be the same Hendrix that Rielle used to work for, could it?

"Yep. Hendrix Marketing, located downtown."

"Get me their info."

"You're serious?" Bill sounds surprised. "I didn't expect you to be interested in a vodka endorsement but I guess with the season coming to an end, it is a good time to diversify your portfolio."

"I'm not taking the deal. No matter what they offer, the answer is no. But I want to be the one to tell them that. Get me the heads of the company and a guy named Stu's contact info."

"This sounds personal, Torst."

I take another sip of my tea, relaxing back into my seat. "It's about as personal as it could get, Bill. We're about to take-off. Call you this week?"

"Sure thing. I'll send you the contact information as soon as I have it."

"Great. Thanks." I hang up the phone and close my eyes.

Hendrix Marketing and specifically Stu, Rielle's ex-boss, are going to learn firsthand why the vodka company and any other brand they're promoting won't have a Hawks player endorsing shit. They messed with the wrong woman, and by extension, the wrong man.

I close my eyes and sleep soundly until we touch down in Boston.

IT'S SUNNY, cold, and early when I step through the door of my apartment, balancing a tray of Starbucks on my palm.

I place the tray on the kitchen island, drop my things in the living room, and grin at Rielle's random belongings scattered throughout the room. A pair of boots next to the living room couch. Sunglasses on the console table. An earmarked paperback of *Little Women* next to the sink. She's settling into her new life. I rub my hands together and check the time. It's before 6 a.m. and I know Rielle won't be up for a while. Even though I should be exhausted after playing two tough games in three days, I'm too restless to go back to sleep. Instead, I decide to cook Rielle breakfast.

Isn't that something good husbands do? Cook?

Besides, it's been a long time since I've had a woman in my apartment that I genuinely *want* to cook for. Grinning to myself, I pull out some ingredients, grateful Missy, my housekeeper, is still ordering the groceries. I doubt Rielle would know how much I like smoked salmon. I whip up scrambled eggs and smoked salmon, piling the combination on top of thick slices of toast. Farmor used to make this for me after my early morning hockey practices. Today, I add my own twist: sliced avocado.

Rielle stumbles into the kitchen fifteen minutes later, her eyes still bleary with sleep and her hair snaking down her back in wild waves. She's so clearly not a morning person and yet, seeing her propped up against the refrigerator, tugging on the hem of the T-shirt that hits her mid-thigh, makes me smile.

"Morning, sunshine." I raise a Starbucks cup to my mouth and nudge the second one closer to her.

"Morning, Torst," she replies, picking up the cup. Her eyes widen, the sleep clearing, when she reads the label. "A caramel macchiato? How'd you know?"

I chuckle, not willing to divulge my sources, aka Claire. "You hungry?"

She takes in the two plates and a little line forms between her eyebrows. "You didn't have to cook breakfast."

"I wanted to. We can go out for lunch or dinner or something," I tack on, knowing I promised we'd actually leave the penthouse and do something together.

Rielle shakes her head. "This is perfect." She slips onto a barstool and I push the plate closer to her.

"Hope you like smoked salmon." I take the seat next to hers.

She nods and takes a bite, moaning as she chews. "This is delicious. Thank you. What time did you get in? I didn't even hear you."

"Not that long ago. How was your last few days here?" I take a bite of my sandwich, my eyes closing as I'm transported back to Farmor's kitchen and my childhood. The closer we get to summer, to seeing Farmor, to saying goodbye, the more my childhood memories rush back.

"Everything's good. I've applied for some jobs, reached out to some alumni at my university to check out positions. I should be able to line up a few interviews, even without a recommendation letter."

"And you're set on marketing?"

She glances up, her eyebrows pulling together. "What do you mean?"

I shrug. "You can do anything you want, Ri. I've heard you're pretty much a marketing guru—"

She snorts and tucks her hair behind her ears.

"But just because you're good at something doesn't mean it's your passion, you know?"

She nods slowly. "You think I should do something else?"

"I think you should explore any option you have interest in and see what you enjoy most. Part of this"—I gesture between us—"is you not having to stay in some unfulfilling job because you need the paycheck. Even though you're being crazy stubborn about the paycheck part."

She snickers and meets my eyes with a sheepish expression on her face. "A girl Claire and I went to school with is a cocktail waitress at Jolene's. She's having surgery and needs to take two weeks off and since they're short-staffed, her boss agreed to let me pick up her shifts since she knows me too. So…" She grins.

I laugh. "You have a short-term cocktail waitressing gig?" She nods.

"And you feel better, knowing you're earning some money?" I surmise.

She nods again, twirling a strand of her hair around her fingers.

"Okay," I say, not admitting I'd rather she just use the freaking credit card in her wallet. But I get that she wants to pay her own way, hell, I even admire it. I take another bite of my sandwich, turning thoughts over in my mind. "But Ri— don't think, just answer—what's your dream job?"

Her eyes flash, diamonds and coal. "Photography."

I straighten, startled by her response. Not because I don't see her behind a camera lens, but part of me didn't expect her to respond so candidly. To be so forthcoming.

She chuckles at my expression. "I took a bunch of courses in college. All electives but I loved them. I loved the assignments and learning different techniques, especially with regards to lighting. My senior year, my class got to set up photoshoots for different 'clients.' It was an opportunity to blend everything I learned through marketing with photography. How to create a set or find a location that would give the desirous effect. We got to weigh in on wardrobe." Her expression takes on a dreamy look, as if she's recalling the assignment. "It was a lot of fun," she says wistfully.

"Who were your clients?"

She laughs, swiping up her coffee cup. It dangles from her fingers like a prop as she moves her hands, becoming more animated. "A newly engaged couple, a little girl's birthday photos, and a family of five wanted just normal, lifestyle photos. Everyone in the class submitted a proposal with their ideas for the shoots and the clients each chose two to three sessions to attend. It was a lot of fun."

"Who did you shoot?" I cross my elbows on the island and lean closer, drawn to this version of Rielle. The uninhibited, honest, excited woman who often hides behind a sly grin and quick eyes.

"The family of five." She grins. "The kids were adorable. We totally had a massive tantrum from the toddler, a little girl named Grace." She shakes her head as if to clear it. "Anyway, they were so happy with how the photos turned out. Two months later, the woman, Chantelle, called me. Her sister was getting married that weekend in a small ceremony and the photographer had come down with mono." She wrinkles her nose.

My mouth pops open, seeing where this is going. "They asked you to photograph the wedding?"

She nods and then laughter drops from her mouth. A delighted, playful laugh. Her eyes crinkle at the corners and right now, with no makeup on and in a threadbare T-shirt, she looks more beautiful than I've ever seen her. "God, Torst, it was the best. I mean, the bride and groom were so gracious of my inexperience, but I had the best day. It's really something, you know, seeing people be so honest with their emotions. So naked and vulnerable." She bites the corner of her mouth, her expression almost melancholy before she blinks and it clears. "Anyway, their pictures turned out better than I expected and I think we were all a little relieved."

"You never considered exploring it further? Photography as a career? Having your own business?" I press, polishing off my sandwich.

Rielle shrugs. "The second I was offered the job at Hendrix, any thoughts about anything flew out the window. I just wanted to pay back Jerry Jensen. To not be drowning in debt."

"And now, you're not," I remind her.

She laughs. "We'll see. I checked out some courses this week—"

"You did?" A buzz zips through my chest. I love seeing Rielle excited about something, interested and eager. It's a good look on anyone but on her, it's mesmerizing.

"Yeah." She shakes her head, trying to play it casual. But I see the spark in her eyes. "They're *expensive*. Not to mention the cost of a camera." She shrugs. "We'll see how well the tips are at Jolene's over the next two weeks."

I snicker, knowing she meant it as a joke. But already, I'm turning over ideas of how to get a camera in her hands without her feeling weird about it. Knowing this conversation is coming to an end and I can't press her anymore this morning, I change the topic.

"Hey, will you come to my game tomorrow?" I ask. "To advance to the next round, it's best of seven. We're up three to two."

"I know." She snorts, shooting me a strange look. "You're my husband, Torsten. I've been following the playoffs."

I dip my head, feeling lighter than I have since our wedding night. I wasn't sure how Rielle and I would manage the intertwining of our lives but right now, it seems natural. "Will you come?"

"I gotta show you something." She scoots from the barstool and leaves the kitchen without answering.

I lean back in my seat and wait for her to return.

When she does, my breath catches and my throat dries. Rielle is rocking my jersey. She does a little twirl and seeing her in my number, with my name stamped across her shoulder blades, affects me on a level I wasn't prepared for. I like seeing her rock my number, wearing my name. I grin. "You look good in my number, sweetheart."

She does a little shimmy that causes us both to laugh.

"Of course I'm coming to your game," she says.

We finish our breakfast and clear off the table together, chatting about regular, normal things. Mostly, our friends. Easton's recovery and Claire's new design business. Indy's pregnancy and how Noah's going to be a crazy helicopter dad.

It's easygoing. Normal. It's something most couples take for granted every day. But eating breakfast with someone whose company I enjoy is nothing to take for granted. It's the best morning I've had in a long time. I smile at Rielle and she grins back and something between us shifts. We share a moment that's so much larger than this instant because it's as if we come to a silent understanding. We're friends, we care about each other's best interests, and right now, that's more than enough.

"SHE LOOKS GOOD IN THAT NUMBER," East bangs his fist against my shoulder in the locker room.

I snicker. "She sitting with Claire?"

He nods. "Everyone is desperate for the details on your wedding, you know? It's not every day everyone's favorite flirt ties the knot."

I shrug. Across the locker room, James watches me carefully. When I meet his eyes, he fixes me with a look. One that says *don't mess this up.* But what no one knows is I have no desire to mess things up with Rielle. Even though a part of me hoped our relationship would evolve into something deeper, right now, I'll take her any way I can get her. And if that's just friendship, then I'm holding on to that with both hands.

We take the ice and I revel in the moment, now savoring every second of play since I know my time is just about up. It's bittersweet and nostalgic and hopeful all at once. I've seen players hang up their skates with misery etched in the lines of their faces and I've watched players hang up their skates with their heads turned to the future, to creating what comes next. I'd rather be the latter and it's definitely a conscious choice, one I have to strive for. Because when I pass the puck to Noah and he makes the first goal of the game, the crowd rushes to their feet. The cheers and noise that ring out is deafening. It's hard to let all that notoriety go after so long. I scan the crowd and when I find Rielle, sitting with the wives and girlfriends, cheering my name and wearing my number, some of the pain eases.

I choose the future, even if it seems more uncertain than an NHL career.

The following weeks pass quickly as Torsten and I settle into our new lives. The Hawks advance to the second round of playoffs and I show up to each of Torsten's home games wearing his jersey with pride. When he's out of town, I pick up extra shifts at Jolene's, socking away any money I can for one of the photography courses I've been researching. My life looks entirely different than it did a handful of weeks ago but if I'm being honest, I'm so much happier.

It's not the penthouse or the financial safety net either. It's Torsten. The way he fills the space with warmth and energy. The way his eyes sometimes smolder when I catch him looking at me. The way he asks about my career plans with genuine interest. I've always known him to be friendly, easygoing, and engaging. But now, I crave the way his eyes find mine when he's on the rink and I'm in the stands. I love the way he smiles at me when I enter the kitchen in the morning. I look forward to curling up next to him on the couch and watching Netflix before bed.

I'm a little enamored with my husband and after the line I drew in the sand, I have no idea how to cross it. I don't want to rock the boat when things between Torsten and me are going so well. But I also don't know how to control the feelings that wash over me when he enters a room, the fantasies of him crawling up my naked body that blare in my mind when he darts out of his bedroom with only a towel around his waist. I've always known marrying Torsten would be dangerous for my heart, but the more time I spend with the Hawks' reformed bachelor, the more I wonder if I'm hurting us both by holding back from what could be a really incredible relationship. A real *marriage.*

"Hey Ri, you working tomorrow night?" he asks when I enter the kitchen, my purse already over my shoulder.

"Nope." I grin at him. "Tonight is actually my last shift because my friend is coming back to work. But the manager added me to a list in case they ever need someone to cover a shift."

"That's pretty cool." He leans back against the countertop. Sweatpants ride low on his hips and the ridges of his abs are visible through the thin material of the tank top he's rocking. His biceps bulge as he crosses his arms over his chest and I think, not for the first time, how damn sexy he is.

"Huh?" I ask, bringing my eyes back to his.

He smirks at me, a knowing glint in his eyes. He shifts his weight to make his muscles pop even more and I feel the blush that works up my cheeks. He totally caught me checking him out. But, I mean, really, how could I not when all that delicious muscle and strength is just *right there,* on full display?

Torsten's eyes twinkle. "I was asking if you wanted to grab drinks with the group tomorrow at Taps? It's going to be very laidback but the team is insisting…"

"On?" I furrow my brow. What the hell are we even talking about?

Torsten's grin widens. "My sweet wife, tomorrow this hunky specimen of pure male"—he rolls his hand down his body, which I drink in appreciatively—"turns thirty-eight."

My eyes snap back to his and my mouth drops open. How

did I not know his birthday? We filled out so much paperwork that clearly stated both of our birthdates and oh my God—"I'm the worst wife ever."

Torsten laughs and shakes his head. "Don't worry about, it's not something I advertise. I mean, I'm getting close to the big four-oh."

My cheeks blaze and I wring my hands together. After everything this man has done for me, I forgot his birthday. "Torsten, I feel awful. Wait, you have to let me—"

"Ri, it's not a big deal. You want to do something nice for me?"

I nod, biting my bottom lip.

"Come to Taps tomorrow."

"Of course I'll be there."

"And do me one favor?" He turns those pale blue eyes on mine, silently begging for me to say yes.

As if I'd say anything else in this moment. "Whatever you want."

"Oh, I like the sound of that," he jokes, pushing off the countertop. He closes the space between us and wraps his arms around my back, caging me in between his arms. It's the closest we've been behind closed doors since the wedding night debacle. Automatically, my heart rate speeds up and hopeful me does a sexy shimmy, hating that rational me has been cockblocking her for weeks now.

I glance up at him and he catches the ends of my hair, playing with the strands.

"There's one thing I want for my birthday," he murmurs, his voice a hell of a lot lower, deeper, than it was when he was standing over by the sink.

I swallow thickly and watch as his eyes cloud over. I shuffle the tiniest bit closer to Torsten, loving the way his arms feel around me. I'm drawn to him and I want him and a part of me hates myself for putting so much distance between us that didn't *need* to be there.

"What is it?" I manage to ask, my voice breathy.

A smile rolls over his face, slow and languid, like a spring breeze. He narrows his eyes and quickly drops a peck to my cheek before dropping his hold and backing away. "You'll see tomorrow. Just remember, you promised to say yes."

"What?"

"I gotta head to the arena now. Have a great last shift, Ri."

I stay in the kitchen until the apartment door closes. Even after Torsten's gone, my heart races, my skin tingles, and I wish that he'd kissed me like he did that first night, when I didn't have to keep my feelings locked down. Although right now, I debate how good of a job I am keeping those feelings secret. Because to anyone paying even a tiny bit of attention, it's pretty obvious that I'm smitten with my husband.

"FOR HE'S A JOLLY GOOD FELLOW" rings out loudly as Torsten's teammates pound on tabletops and whistle loudly.

"Happy birthday, Big Daddy!" Claire cheers, approaching the table with two pitchers of beer.

Behind her, I balance a tray of Patron shots on my hand and a few of the guys groan.

"Just one shot! For his birthday," I tell them.

They all acquiesce, knowing Torsten is the king of shots. No one, save for Indy, is getting out of the back room of Taps without downing at least one tequila shot. I pass out the glasses and when I set one down in front of Torsten, he catches my wrist and tugs until I'm perched in his lap.

I don't know if it's because it's his birthday and he's feeling playful, or if he wants to put on a show in front of his teammates, or if he really just wants me in his lap, but I don't protest. At all. In fact, I shimmy my ass until it's pressed against his groin and lean back against the muscled planes of his chest.

The whistles ring out around us but I don't care. Across the table, one of Torsten's teammates, James, watches me curiously. As soon as I make eye contact, he averts his gaze. But I can't think too much about it because in the next moment, the team chant has shifted.

"Kiss her! Kiss her!" These brawny hockey players demand like little boys.

Claire's mouth drops open but she joins the chant, my traitorous best friend. Indy cracks up, one hand covering her mouth, the other resting on her baby bump.

Torsten shifts behind me, his hand covers my thigh, and he leans forward. "Guys, guys. Simmer down. Ri and I—" he tries to formulate a response that will let us graciously bow out of a public smooch.

But after getting married, a little kiss isn't going to stand in the way of showing everyone what we want, what we need, them to believe. Besides, I'd be lying my ass off if I said I didn't actually want to kiss Torsten. As if it hasn't been the only thing I've been fantasizing about for the past week. Well, not the *only* thing but…

I turn into him until my breasts drag across his chest. His eyes widen in surprise but the corners of his mouth curl upwards. Before he can say anything, I kiss him. I kiss him hard. Boldly. With certainty. As if I belong to him and he belongs to me.

Torsten's hands wrap around my upper arms and hold me steady as I deepen the kiss, slanting my mouth over his and pressing against him. He leans back, his one hand cupping my cheek as his tongue demands more from mine. For a second, we duel for command but at the same time, we both settle into the moment, our tongues touching, our hearts racing, and our bodies melting together.

"Get a room!" Panda shouts, throwing straw wrappers at us.

I laugh and pull back, noting the surprise mixed with wonder in Torsten's eyes. He definitely wasn't expecting that. To be honest, neither was I. I could play it off as a birthday kiss, or wanting to show his team that we're for real, but I don't want to lie. I want to be honest with him and admit that I want to give him a thousand more kisses. That I'm starting to fall for his easygoing charm and big heart. I keep holding myself back because I already know that when we divorce, it will gut me. But what if it never comes to that? What if Torsten and I find a way to make our marriage real? What if he wants what I want?

I shoot him a grin and turn back to the table. Claire's eyebrows are up in her hairline and Indy's mouth has dropped open. "Birthday shots!" I remind everyone, shifting the attention back to the reason we're all here.

It works and in the next minute, we're cheersing to Torsten's good health and tossing back tequila. It burns and warms on the way down and I snuggle back up against Torsten's body, realizing there's nowhere else I'd rather be.

We stay at Taps for another hour, everyone laughing and joking and celebrating the birthday boy. But since the Hawks have a game tomorrow, Austin claps his hands and calls the night early. On her way out the door, Claire turns to glance at me over her shoulder. She holds her hand to her ear in the symbol of a phone and shakes it, letting me know she knows that kiss was for real, and we are most definitely going to talk about it.

I grin and nod at her, feeling too giddy to be ashamed.

Torsten slips his hand in mine and links our fingers together as we leave Taps and walk to his car. Even after we're away from prying eyes, he holds my hand and a warm thrill shoots through me.

We drive back to his place and he glances at me from the corner of his eye. "You have fun tonight?"

I nod. "Happy birthday, Torst."

"I'm an old man, Ri."

"You're a sexy man," I tell him, taking a big step out on the limb I'm desperate to run across.

He licks his lips, a cocky smirk glancing off his mouth. "You think I'm sexy?"

I snort, turning to glance out the window so he won't see me blush.

We park at his building and take the elevator up to the penthouse. When we cross the threshold, I hold up one finger. "Hold up, I have something for you." I dart to my room to retrieve the gift I bought him this morning. Even though it took a sizable chunk out of my photography course savings, I didn't think twice about buying it.

When I enter the living room, his eyes widen as he takes in the wrapped present held between my hands.

"You got me a gift?" he asks the obvious and I nod, passing it to him.

"Happy birthday."

"Sweetheart"—he turns the package over in his hands—"you didn't have to do this, Ri."

"You don't even know what it is. You might hate it."

He gives me a look and unwraps the present. He breathes in sharply as he studies the delicate cuff links. They're hockey sticks, crossed at the center. Nothing fancy, just sterling silver, but when I saw them, they reminded me of him. "Rielle, you didn't have to buy me anything. This, being with you right now on my birthday, is more than enough."

I wave a hand dismissively. "It's nothing. I thought maybe you could wear them for your away games. Know I'm with you even if I'm not physically with you."

"It's not nothing. It's thoughtful," he murmurs, his eyes

catching mine. "Thank you." His voice is sincere and it warms my chest.

I smile and take a step closer.

He sets down my present and reaches onto the couch for something. "Close your eyes."

"Wait, what?"

He lifts an eyebrow at me. "You promised."

Yesterday's conversation comes back to me and I laugh, closing my eyes like he requested.

"Hold out your hands."

I do as he says, wondering what he's up to.

He places something in my hands. It's heavier than I expected.

"Open them."

I open my eyes and glance down at a brand new DSLR camera. I gasp, "Torsten!"

He watches me closely. "Do you like it?"

"I love it. Are you crazy? This costs a—"

"Your photography course starts in a week. You need a camera for it."

My mouth drops open. "This is too much," I protest, trying to give the camera back to him.

He holds up his hands and shakes his head. "No way. You promised, babe. This is what I want for my birthday."

"To give someone else a gift?" I ask, both overwhelmed by his generosity and so freaking touched by the thoughtfulness behind it.

"To see you do something you love," he clarifies.

I place the camera down and step in between his thighs, where he's seated on the armrest of the couch. Hesitantly, my hands lift and rest on the tops of his shoulders. "It's still too much."

"Trust me, the things I want for you…" He shakes his head. "This is nothing."

"Torsten," I murmur, unsure what I want to say next.

His hands find my hips and settle there. "That kiss at Taps, was it for real, Rielle?"

The moment of truth. I hesitate and his eyes begin to shudder closed.

"It was for real," I rush to explain.

Torsten's head snaps up and his eyes bore into mine, colored in hope and skepticism.

I wince at the mixed messages I've been sending, seeing the uncertainty in his gaze.

"I've wanted to kiss you for weeks. Since before we even got married," I admit, laughing lightly. But Torsten's features are locked down. His hands grip me a little tighter but he doesn't say anything so I continue. "I don't know how to do this with you and not end up hurt or worse, hurting you," I whisper, licking my bottom lip.

"You think me hurting would be worse than you hurting?" he murmurs.

I nod.

Torsten's expression softens, the tenderness I recall from our first night together swelling in his eyes. It's so honest, so brave, that I shuffle even closer.

His hand moves up my body, cupping my cheek. He stares into my eyes, and for a beat, we have an entire conversation without any words. It's as if we're standing on a cliff and we both know that if we take this step, we're going to tumble over the edge. We just don't know how far the fall is or what perils wait for us when we land.

I lick my bottom lip in anticipation, in nerves, in want.

Slowly, Torsten closes the space between our mouths. I meet him halfway.

And when our lips finally touch, we kiss each other like it's both the first time and like we've been doing it for decades. It's heady, pulling me under completely. But it's also hesitant, a testing of the waters rather than a losing of control.

Torsten is the first to pull away and the emotion in his

eyes crashes over me like a wave. He searches my eyes, looking for confirmation. I lean forward and press my lips to his, letting him know that I want this. I want him. We jump off the cliff and freefall.

Torsten lifts me and I wrap my legs around his hips. He walks us slowly to his bedroom, stopping when we're in the doorframe. His hips pin mine to the wall, his hands wrapped around the backs of my thighs, supporting my weight. He pulls back slightly, his eyes finding mine. "I don't want to rush anything with you, Ri. I don't want you to feel confused about me, about us. I respect the hell out of you, sweetheart."

His words are extra reassurances I appreciate, but don't need. Because I already made up my mind tonight, watching him at Taps. "I want to try with you, Torsten. Me and you, for real."

His eyes widen and drop to my lips before slamming back into mine. "You sure, Ri? Because once you're mine...I won't just let you go."

My heart is racing. It's beating so loudly, I'm sure he can hear it. My legs start to tremble and my fingers dig into his shoulders to steady myself. "Promise?"

He doesn't respond because his restraint slips at my response. Torsten's lips crash over mine. He kisses me fiercely, with a hint of possessiveness that wasn't there before. I revel in it, meeting him kiss for kiss as he jerks us away from the doorframe and relocates us to his bed.

I flop down in the center of his mattress, shimmying out of my jeans and whipping my sweater over my head. Torsten quickly loses his clothes too. His body covers mine and he pauses. He hovers over me, our eyes meeting and holding. Torsten slowly lowers his face and I lift my chin. Our mouths touch again and this time, our kiss is slow. It's deep and sensual and causes a swell of emotion to trail through my limbs and a rush of heat to flow between my legs.

My hands track the planes of his back, grazing over his

rippling muscles, and pulling him closer. He explores my body like it's a marvel, his fingers and mouth touching every inch of my skin. We lose ourselves in each other, in this moment, touching and tasting, reveling and cherishing. When Torsten shifts away to grab a condom from his bedside table, I clasp his wrist and shake my head.

"I'm on the pill."

He freezes, his eyes drinking me in. "Sweetheart, are you—"

"I'm sure, Torst."

He inches closer to me, his hand brushing my hair away from my face, his fingers grazing the curve of my shoulder. "I'm clean, sweetheart. I've never not used a condom."

"Me too. And I haven't either," I reassure him. I've always been safe. I've never let myself get this emotionally involved with anyone before and it feels different. All the physical acts of pleasure feel deeper, more, now that I'm emotionally invested.

Torsten's hands cup my face and he kisses me reverently, guiding my head back to the pillows. He kisses me like he'll never get enough as he slides inside of me. I gasp as he fills me, my hands clenching at his ribs. He pulls back and watches me, his gaze intense, as our bodies join together.

When he's in all the way, he stills, and the sound of our breathing fills the air.

"You mean everything to me, Ri," he murmurs, starting to move.

I groan as he drags out of me slowly before pushing back in. My body stretches to accommodate him, and delicious sensations rock through me. "Don't stop, Torst," I gasp as everything tightens. He sets a steady pace and slowly, pressure builds and my limbs tighten. My toes curl and my back arches off the bed. "Torsten!" I shatter around him, having the most intense orgasm of my life.

Torsten rides my pleasure, his eyes boring into mine.

I grasp his face, looking straight at him as I admit, "I'm falling for you, Torst."

He swears and pumps into me faster, setting a relentless pace, until he gasps out my name and collapses on top of me.

I hug him close as he begins to soften inside of me. Our ragged breathing settles and Torsten slips out of me, curling his body protectively around mine. He tucks some of my hair behind my ear. His thumb drags along my lower lip, tracing my features. I turn to stare at him, feeling sated and relaxed and deliriously happy.

He smiles at me, leaning forward to kiss me deeply.

"I've been falling for you for a long time, Ri."

I smile back. "You think we can do this?"

He nods, pulling his duvet cover over our naked bodies. "Yeah. We take it one day at a time."

"Okay," I agree, pressing a quick peck to his mouth.

"Okay," he says, pulling me back until I rest against his chest. He wraps his arm around my middle and links our fingers together.

I snuggle into his warmth.

"Best birthday of my life," he murmurs in my ear.

I chuckle, wiggling my ass against him. "You really are old," I joke.

He pinches my side and I giggle. Slowly, sleep falls over us and I close my eyes, finally feeling like I found my home.

CHAPTER FOURTEEN
TORSTEN

"**M**r. Hansen, we're so grateful you wanted to come in to meet with us." Josh Hendrix, the grandson of John Hendrix, founder of Hendrix Marketing, shakes my hand enthusiastically.

"Thanks for having me," I say, offering him a grin.

We take a seat at a conference room table as Josh introduces me to a handful of men, one of them being Stu Sanders. Bingo. It figures there's not a woman in the room. I lean back in my chair and study each of the men. "Tell me about the vodka."

"We're really enthusiastic about working with Saint Vodka and love the idea of having athletes, such as yourself, represent the brand." Josh launches into his sales pitch, telling me all about Saint, about Hendrix's marketing vision, about shooting a commercial, yada, yada.

But my focus is trained on Stu Sanders, who must pick up on my vibe, because about a third of the way into Josh's little speech, Stu starts shooting me worried looks.

I smile, feigning politeness when I really want to reach across the table, grab him by his collar, and demand to know every inappropriate time he touched, spoke to, or thought about my *wife*. The thought leaves me reeling because yes, Rielle is my wife. But God, she's so much more than that. Over the past few weeks, she's become my…everything. My sounding board, my advice-giver, my shoulder to lean on, my ride or freaking die. The little prick scared to make eye contact with me deserves a hell of a lot more than my fist to his face and it pains me that today, I can't even do that. Because, playoffs.

But I can clap my hands when Josh is finished speaking, sit straighter in my seat, and chuckle. "It sounds like a great product. Really, it's definitely something I would order at the bar. I like the direction you're going in too. The athletic component, the moody, gritty, masculine vibe. I wish I could say yes to the endorsement opportunity."

Josh's mouth opens and closes twice before he sputters, "What do you mean? Why can't you sign on? Your agent and lawyer didn't see any type of conflict of interest."

"It's personal." I glare at Stu Sanders, narrowing my eyes. "I believe my wife used to work for you, under Stu over here."

Stu visibly pales, his eyes nearly falling out of his head.

I lean closer, my voice quiet, laced with all the threats I'm not at liberty to openly throw at him. "Name Rielle Carter ring a bell?"

He drops his head and moves to stand from his chair.

"Sit back down," I bellow, my restraint snapping.

"Now, now," Josh mutters, stepping toward the conference table with his hands raised. "I'm sure there's some kind of misunderstanding—"

"Why don't you tell your boss, all the men in this room, how there wasn't a misunderstanding. How you took advantage of my wife's work ethic for months before sexually assaulting her." I keep my eyes trained on Stu for a long moment. The atmosphere in the room drops to freezing, everyone around the conference table shifting uncomfortably in their chairs. Good. They should be uncomfortable. I glance around the table. "Unless you all knew about it and—"

"No, no. God, no. Of course not." Josh shakes his head, looking truly disturbed at my words. "Stu?"

Stu's hands are shaking and he looks like he's about to have a heart attack. I lean back in my chair and cross my arms over my chest, waiting.

He licks his cracked lips nervously, his beady eyes almost tearing up.

I lift my eyebrows. *We're fucking waiting, Stu.*

"I didn't mean—" he starts.

I frown.

"I thought Rielle—"

"Try again," I snap.

"I'm sorry for putting my hands on Rielle," he mumbles.

"My *wife*."

"Your wife," he repeats, his eyes drawn to the carpet.

"And...?" I prompt.

"I never should have said the things I said to her or done the things I did." His shoulders slump and I want to kick him in the balls so hard, they'll come up out of his mouth.

My hands clench into fists as I try to control my accelerated breathing. Just hearing him say those words, imagining the things he *said* and *did* to Rielle, has me seeing red.

I glare at Josh who, thankfully, can read a room a hell of a lot better than Stu.

"We'll be launching an investigation into Stu Sanders' relationship—"

I clear my throat harshly.

Josh amends his statement, "treatment of Ms. Carter."

"Mrs. Hansen," I correct. "Immediately."

Josh nods as Stu shuffles around nervously, unsure whether to stay or go. What a dick.

I stand from my chair. "Well, gentlemen, it was nice to meet all of you today. Too bad it couldn't be under more pleasant circumstances. As a result of that man's"—I point to Stu—"disgusting, revolting, not to mention illegal actions, I take great pleasure in letting you know that no members of the Hawks franchise will be signing any endorsement deal with your marketing firm, to represent Saint or any other product you have. What happens next, regarding the legal and professional actions taken against Stu, will determine just how much I share this story with other athletes, both in hockey and in other sports. Thank you for your time." I stride to the conference room door, keeping my head straight ahead. Right before I reach the handle, I snap my fingers and turn back to the room. "Oh and since Rielle was fired for *not* sleeping with Stu, she needs a letter of recommendation. A glowing one that highlights her more than proficient qualities and high standards of professionalism while working here."

Josh clears his throat, glaring directly at Stu. "I'll take care of it personally. I'll email it today."

"Glad to hear it." I nod once and push out of the office.

I wave to the receptionist as I pass by her desk, smile politely to a man I pass on the way to the elevators, and head to my SUV.

Once I'm behind the wheel, I let out a deep breath and pull my ride to the front of the building where I can get a clear view on who's coming and going.

Not twenty minutes later, a red-faced Stu Sanders pushes out into the daylight, carrying a box with a potted plant and some binders.

Then, I laugh. I laugh until I cry because it feels so fucking good.

"YOU LOOK sexy rocking my number, sweetheart," I tell Ri as I get ready to head to the arena.

She laughs, shakes her ass, and waves her phone in the air. "You're never going to believe what happened!" Her black eyes are glittering and her smile is wide. She's practically glowing with delight.

"What?"

"Stu was fired! Torsten, Hendrix *fired* him. The CEO, Josh, called me personally to apologize *and* sent me over an amazing letter of recommendation." She whoops, throwing her arms out wide. "Can you believe it?"

I stand from zipping up my bag and walk to her, wrapping my arms around her waist and threading them at the base of her spine. "That's incredible, Ri. That piece of shit deserves more than just being fired."

"I know. I'm still trying to figure out how the hell Hendrix even learned about it. Maybe other women came forward? I should have come forward… I didn't even think to press charges." She worries her bottom lip between her teeth and I tug her closer, wrapping my arms around her shoulders in a hug.

"You had a lot going on, babe. Trying to survive the way you were isn't easy. At least you know he's out of a job. I can check around and see what legal action is being taken against him. If you want, you can file something now. We can go to the station together." I glance down at her.

She's chewing her lip raw. I grasp her chin until she releases her lip, her big eyes coming up to meet mine. She hesitates and I press a kiss to her forehead. Slowly, she nods. "You'll really come with me?"

Her worry guts me and I pull her closer. "Of course I will, baby. I'm one hundred percent behind whatever you want to do. But I should tell you that Hendrix offered me an endorsement deal."

She jerks back, stepping away from me. "They did?"

"I met with Josh and his team today."

"Was Stu there?"

I growl at hearing his name on her lips. My hands clench into fists and my molars grind together, recalling his beady eyes and the fear that flared in them when he realized who the hell I am and my connection to Rielle.

Realization dawns in her expression and she gasps. "It was you. You got him fired."

I reach for her again, some of the fury racing through me quieting once my skin connects with hers.

She shakes her head in disbelief. "You turned down an endorsement deal? For me? Now, when you're about to retire and should be diversifying your portfolio?"

"Sweetheart, when are you going to realize I'd do anything for you? Turning down a deal is nothing when it comes to your safety. Your well-being. Of any woman's well-being."

Her hands find my shoulders and she presses up onto her tippy toes to brush her lips against mine. Immediately, I'm dragged under her spell. My hands settle on her hips as I deepen our connection. Will I ever get enough of this woman? God, I hope not.

When she pulls back, she looks at me in awe, like I did something worth a damn. Her reverence fills me with pride and a possessiveness; a desire to always protect her streaks through me.

"Thank you, Torsten."

I brush my thumb along her cheekbone. "Don't thank me, sweetheart. Just know that you're safe, he's gone, and you have a letter of recommendation. I feel better that you're here, with me, where I can keep an eye on things."

She lifts an eyebrow. "Keep an eye on things?"

I chuckle. "On you, Ri. Keep an eye on you. Now, I've gotta get to the arena. See you at the game?"

She rolls her eyes. "As if I'd miss it."

I grin, press a light kiss to the corner of her mouth, and shoulder my bag.

When I arrive at the arena, I spend an extra minute in the car, watching other people walk toward the place that's been home to me for nearly two decades. I've spent more hours in this place than I have in my own home.

It's a bittersweet feeling, knowing that in a handful of weeks, I'll no longer enter it as a Hawks player. I climb from my SUV and head inside. For the second round, we're facing off against the New York Sharks. Despite their fierce competition, a few of the Sharks used to play for the Hawks, including Austin's brother-in-law, Mike. It must make things a little awkward around the Merrick family dining table, but right now, I need to get my head on straight and prepare for the game.

I run through all of my usual pre-game traditions but add a new one. I take an extra moment to rattle the cuff links Rielle bought me in my palm before placing them on the top shelf of my locker.

When I glide onto the ice, I glance to the WAGs box until my eyes find Rielle's. She's staring straight at me, a goofy grin on her face. She blows me a kiss and I smile, winking at her. A few of the women sitting near her practically swoon and Claire rolls her eyes.

But I know Ri didn't do it for show. She's rooting for me, for the team, for us.

A sense of pride and a swell of peace washes over me as I line up for the face-off. I vow to make each second on the ice count. But my play is cut short. We're only four minutes into the game when I collide with the Shark's center and hear my shoulder pop. Pain rips through my arm. The cool air rushes past my visor as I go down. My knee connects with the ice and it's like landing on a grenade. I feel the vibrations ricochet throughout my body. My torso twists as I throw my good arm out in an attempt to slow my fall. But it's too late. My head bounces off the ice, my body goes slack, and pain sears through me.

A flash of color. A cool breeze. A loud yell.

Then, darkness.

"Don't move it. Here, I got you," I chatter on and on, gently guiding Torsten as we maneuver into the penthouse.

My heart is still galloping and I can't stop the adrenaline that pumps in my temples. Seeing him go down tonight was the most horrible thing I've ever witnessed. Helplessness gripped me as I leapt to my feet, my heart in my throat, my knees weak, my legs shaking. A buzzing sound rung in my ears and if it wasn't for Claire and Indy pulling me out of the box, I may have passed out right there.

Fortunately, the fall looked a lot worse than it was. Torsten came to only seconds after blacking out. He had a dislocated shoulder, which the doctor was able to pop back in, a beat-up knee which is causing him some pain, and a mild concussion. But the doctor cleared him to come home, so here we are. Me, propping Torsten up and chatting a million miles a minute to eat up the silence that has ensued since the moment I walked into the trainer's room and saw Torsten laid out on the table.

His eyes are stormy, his mouth twisted in pain and anger, his mind somewhere else entirely. For the first time since we've entered into our arrangement, I can't get a word out of him. He's looking through me instead of at me. Of course, the logical part of my brain recognizes that he's in physical pain. Not to mention, the emotional distress of knowing that tonight was most likely his last game as an NHL player. But the emotional side of me can't help but worry that something just fundamentally shifted.

"Here we are." I ease him down onto the couch. Bending to pick up his leg so I can prop it on the coffee table, he swats at me.

"Leave it. I'm not an invalid."

"I know that. I'm just trying to help you," I say in the most even voice I can manage. Images of him going down replay in my mind and with every blink, I recall more details. The unnatural twist of his body, the shocked faces of the crowd, the deafening silence of thousands of people holding their breaths in unison. The arena felt suffocating and I couldn't wait to come home with Torsten but now that we're here, my nerves are scattered.

I watch him struggle to lift his leg on his own and back away slowly to gather ice packs from the kitchen. When I return, Torsten gives me a smirk and glances at his leg, which is neatly stacked on the coffee table.

"Here's some ice."

"Thanks," he mutters, taking the wrapped packs and bag from me and placing them where he needs to.

"Do you want to talk about it?"

He lifts an eyebrow at me, his expression carefully neutral. But his eyes swirl and churn, angry and hurting and glinting with something I've never seen before. "What do you think?"

I bite my lip and shake my head.

Torsten mutters out a string of colorful language and opens his hand for mine. When I place my hand in his, he tugs until I'm seated next to him on the couch.

"I'm sorry, Ri. Look, I'm fucking pissed right now. It has nothing to do with you. I'm just—fuck!" He picks up the remote control and slings it across the room. It bounces twice on the floor before skittering to a stop near the step up to the kitchen. "I can't believe that's how my fucking career ends. That pathetic, garbage play. Dropping like that and blacking out like a fucking pussy. I'm angry. And I'm...I'm heartbroken."

"I'm sorry, Torst." I squeeze his hand to let him know I'm here, that I'm listening.

He heaves out a sigh. "I just want to sit here and watch shitty TV."

"Are you hungry?"

He shakes his head.

"Do you want some company?" I ask pathetically, desperate for him to say yes. Even though he might want some time on his own, the thought of leaving him alone to hurt by himself aches.

He shifts his weight so he can wrap his arm around my shoulders.

I immediately curl into his side, my palm on his chest, my head on his good shoulder. I lean up and press a kiss to his cheek. "I'm just going to get the remote control. Don't move."

He groans and tosses his head back but a smirk glances off his mouth.

"Too soon?" I guess, hopping from the couch to grab the remote.

"Get your ass back here, Ri." He takes the remote from my hand as I settle back beside him. He turns on the TV. "*Schitt's Creek?*"

"Duh." It's pretty much become our nightly staple. After sex, I mean.

He snorts and pulls me closer. I go willingly, breathing in the scent of him, sweat and man and a hint of body wash. His fingers rake through my hair, grazing lazily against my back. I sink deeper into his side, my eyes glued to the television.

Each of his inhales draws me closer and I sit perfectly still, aware of every shift he makes. The air around us intensifies, layers of unspoken words, desperate thoughts, and needy desires, building like the pressure in a volcano. Torsten's fingers stroke lower, his hand wrapping around the side of my body, splaying wide along my rib cage.

I suck my stomach in, feeling the boldness in his touch. Am I what he needs right now? Does he crave a distraction? A release?

Is it because of the devasting blows he took tonight? Both physically and mentally? Or is it more than that? Is it because even though we never intended to, we're becoming a "we," and right now, I can soothe some of his hurt?

I turn more into him, my breasts skimming against his chest. He inhales sharply and turns his face to mine, his eyes darker than I've ever seen them. The anguish lining his face, the bitterness in the clench of his jaw, has my hand sliding up his chest, around his neck, and to the side of his face. His eyes close and his nostrils flare.

He turns his face into my touch and drags his lips over my palm. "Rielle," he murmurs. I love the way my name sounds when he says it, but right now, I can't make out any of the emotions twisted in his tone.

All I know is he's hurting and it's making me ache.

He needs comfort and I want nothing more than to provide it.

He's my husband and I'm his wife.

I turn and get my knees underneath me, gingerly swinging a leg over his torso until I'm straddling his hips. Careful to keep my weight off of his injuries, I grip his face in my hands and look into his eyes.

"Tell me what you want, Torst. Don't think, just say it," I throw one of his favorite lines back at him and a spark of recognition flares in his irises.

"You," he murmurs. "Fuck, I need you, Ri."

I slide my hands down until they're flat against his pecs. His muscles ripple under my touch and the fact that this man is thirty-eight and has the body of a twenty-two-year-old, wisdom of a septuagenarian, and the overflowing, brimming heart of a child isn't lost on me. He's the best of every season of life, all rolled into one devastating man.

A spark gleams in his eyes as I lower my head to his and press our lips together. Torsten sighs, his one hand cupping my cheek, the other resting on my hip, holding me steady as I press against him and deepen our connection.

His tongue slips inside my mouth and I moan, all the delicious sensations from our nights together culminating in this moment. There's an added layer of trust between us that makes every touch deeper, each kiss sweeter. His hand threads through my hair as he tries to sit up and take control of the kiss.

I shake my head, pulling back to grin at him. "Uh-uh. You're the patient. Let me." I bite my bottom lip, reaching for the tie of his sweatpants.

He half groans, half chuckles, dropping his head back to look to the ceiling, as if for patience. Or strength. Either way, I set to work and shimmy his pants off his hips. Then, I sink to my knees, in the space between his propped leg and his other foot which is bouncing against the floor. I place my hand over the top of his foot to stop the bouncing and he snorts.

"You nervous?" I ask coyly.

"Nervous I'm not going to last," he admits, glancing down at me. "Seeing you like this is enough to put me over the edge."

I chuckle and pull the impressive tent he's already pitching out of his boxers. My hand wraps around his heated skin, silky and already rock hard. I sigh, loving the feel of him, the weight of his need, against my palm.

I stroke him from shaft to tip, pressing kisses along his inner thigh. The closer I inch toward him, the more I let my tongue slip and swirl against his skin. He hardens even more in my hand, his breathing growing ragged.

My heart is pounding at how much I affect him. Torsten's reputation has always preceded him but right now, he seems nothing like the perpetual bachelor. Instead, he seems like a man warring with himself to keep it together. I like that I affect him so deeply, especially since it's been years since I've given a shit one way or the other how I make a man feel. Sex has always been a casual exchange for me.

But since Torsten, it's almost too much. Even though my touch is sure, my mind is overflowing with thoughts. And pleas to a higher being that I can make this as spectacular for him as he makes every single thing for me. I lick up his shaft before putting my lips around him. He swears as I begin to bob my head, his fingers lacing through my hair, massaging my scalp. I switch up the pace, alternating between fast and slow, deep and shallow, and he groans, his thigh tightening under my hand. I don't know how much time passes because I'm so focused on making this good for him, that everything except the feel of his length, the heat of his skin, his groans filling the air, disappear.

His hands tighten in my hair. "Ri, fuck baby, that's good."

I hollow out my cheeks, taking him until he hits the back of my throat, and he swears, tugging on my hair.

"Baby, I'm gonna—"

He explodes in my mouth, sticky, salty ribbons of pleasure that I swallow without a second thought, taking an extra moment to lick him clean while his hand wraps around my arm and tries to pull me up.

When I lift my eyes to his, he's staring at me in awe. "Rielle, you didn't have to—"

"I wanted to," I cut him off.

"Come here." He motions for me and I climb back into his lap.

He winces as my foot catches on his injured knee and I freeze. "Sorry. I didn't mean—"

"Shh," he cuts me off, gripping my waist and pulling until

I collapse against his chest and he presses the deepest, dirtiest kiss to my mouth. "I don't know what I did to deserve you, this, but fuck, Rielle, I'm happy you're here. And it's got nothing to do with—" He lifts his chin toward his cock, which is already starting to harden for round two.

I snort and he blushes, endearing me to him further.

"Well, maybe not nothing," he amends. He wraps his good arm around my waist and tries to roll me but I hold firm.

"No." I shake my head. "Tonight's about you."

He freezes, his eyes dropping to the button on my jeans. "Sweetheart, I'm not going to leave you hanging like that."

I laugh and stand from his lap, popping open my jeans and shimmying out of them. I pulled off his jersey when we first came through the door. Now, clad in just a black camisole and lace panties, I grin. "I promise, you're not. I wanted to do this, to make you feel good. Come on, let's shower."

His eyes widen further.

"You won't be able to manage on your own and if you play nice, I'll let you soap me up." I waggle my eyebrows and he chuckles.

I lead him to the bathroom and flip on the shower. As we wait for the water to warm, I slowly undress him, careful not to rattle his shoulder or knee. He watches me, his gaze intense, his eyes dark like sapphires. It's intoxicating, the feel of his gaze on my heated skin. Even now, injured and hurting, he makes me feel worshipped with just a glance.

Once the shower water is hot, we step inside. The water beats down on us and my hair sticks to my back and shoulders in thick clumps. Torsten moves his injured arm awkwardly, trying to brush my hair away from my face, his other hand braced against the shower tiles. "You're so goddamn beautiful, Rielle."

"So are you, Torst."

He snorts and closes his eyes. When he opens them, I see

all the hopes and fears he keeps buried beneath his good-time charm, his easygoing vibe, his desire to be well-liked. I step into his frame and kiss him hard.

We make out like teenagers, fumbling around his injuries, quelling our own insecurities that rise to the surface, shifting our normal into new territory. The next level, a new layer, of our deepening relationship.

When I help Torsten into bed, I climb on top of him. Our bodies, naked and still damp from our shower, glisten in the light from the bathroom. I can make out Torsten's features, the shadows that play over our skin.

I lace our fingers together and bring our joined hands up, over his head. I line him up at my entrance before sinking down. He throws his head back and groans. I whimper as he stretches me, filling me completely. My hands slip from his and my palms find his chest. With careful movements, I ride him, slow and deep. Our eyes connect and the vulnerability, the trust, that sparks in Torsten's gaze is my undoing. We both break apart, filling the dark with our mutual desires. Once we're cleaned up, Torsten reaches for me, wraps his arm around my waist, and hauls me next to him. Curled up against him, the rise and fall of his chest, the steady drum of his heartbeat, lulls me to sleep.

I dream of our future. Together.

The shrill ringing of my cell phone wakes us both up at a quarter past three in the morning. I fumble for my phone, swearing as pain shoots through my shoulder.

Rielle moves quickly, swiping my phone from the end table. She flips on the lamp as she passes it to me. The moment I read Farmor's name on the screen, the pain in my arm dissipates and dread weighs heavily in my chest.

I swipe right. "Farmor?"

"It's me," my father's voice comes through the line and I freeze. I haven't heard it in more than five years and still, just two words, bring me back to my childhood. To the nights his eyes would bore into mine with disappointment bordering on hatred. To the day he told me he was done with me, that the family was done with me, since I never showed any of them my respect or loyalty.

Since I chose a *game*, hockey, over them.

"Where's Farmor?" I whisper, clutching the phone so tightly, my hand aches and I briefly wonder if the phone will snap.

Rielle's wide awake now, watching me with curious eyes.

My father clears his throat. "She's in the hospital. I'm only calling because she asked me to. If you want to say goodbye, you better get on a plane." He rattles off the details of the hospital and disconnects the call before I have a chance to respond.

I sit in shock, a million questions ricocheting in my mind. *Is she stable? Is she conscious? Are they taking good care of her? Will I make it in time? What about the playoffs?*

"Torsten?" Rielle touches my hand. "What is it?"

I look at her, my mouth opening and closing several times but no sound comes out. My chest tightens and my head pounds. A barrage of memories, a flood of moments, an entire lifetime of being loved by a good woman race through me, shocking my system further. Farmor is dying.

"Torst?" Rielle grips my fingers now, concern blazing in her black eyes.

"It's my," my voice cracks and I clear my throat. "My farmor. Rielle, I need to go home."

"To Norway?" she whispers, understanding dawning in her expression.

I nod.

"Okay," she says quietly. "Okay." Her gaze scans my room, as if looking for answers to unasked questions.

"I need to be on the next plane. I need to say goodbye." I try to shift from my bed, my knee groaning in protest, my shoulder burning. I swear and sit at the edge of my mattress, trying to muster the physical strength, the mental clarity, to make the next series of decisions.

Rielle hands me my phone. "Call Austin. I'll take care of everything else."

I glance up at her, my brow furrowing. Who is this woman? Who is this beautiful woman brimming with wild passion and deep understanding? How did I end up with a heart like hers?

"Call him," she murmurs, wrapping my fingers around the phone.

I glance down at the screen. My fingers feel thick, uncoordinated, as I find Austin's name and press send.

While I wait for him to answer, Rielle springs into action. She darts to the kitchen and I hear her fingers flying across the keyboard of her laptop just as Austin says, "Hello?"

"Aus, it's me."

"Torst? Fuck, dude, it's after three." I hear him murmur something, a woman's voice travels through the line, and I cringe. Did I interrupt him? Is he dating someone? He clears his throat and when he speaks again, some of the sleep is gone from his voice. "What's going on? You okay?"

"Austin, my grandmother..." I trail off, unsure what to say next.

Austin sighs, "Shit, dude. I'm so fucking sorry. I know how much—"

"I need to go home."

"For the funeral?" he guesses.

"To say goodbye," I clarify, my stomach twisting at the words. Each time I say them, the more real they become. A reality I never wanted to address.

Austin must put together the incomplete puzzle pieces I'm giving him because he says, "Of course. What can I do? When do you leave?"

"As soon as possible. I know we're in New York on—"

"Don't worry about that now, man. You took a big hit tonight, you've got a lot going on, and Greta, she's like your—"

"Family," I murmur. She's my only family that matters. She's more than a grandmother, more than a mother or a father or a brother. For the last three decades of my life, ever since my mother left, she's been all of them rolled into one. "She's all I've got."

"Go to Oslo. Say whatever you need to say. Find your closure, man. The playoffs will be here when you get back.

And as much as I hate to say it, you won't be playing in them anyway, Torst. Not after tonight."

Another reality that cuts deep. No more Farmor, no more hockey, no more anything I recognize.

"Is Rielle going with you?" Austin asks.

I glance up as Rielle flies back into my bedroom, rushing into my closet and coming out with a handful of my clothes.

"I don't know," I say. *Is she? Can she? Will she?*

"You shouldn't be alone right now, man. You know if we weren't in the playoffs, I'd be in the seat next to yours on that flight."

I let out a dry chuckle and nod, even though he can't see me. My fingers pinch the space between my eyes. "I know." I know Austin means it too. He's more than just a captain, he's a true leader on and off the rink. "You have a team to lead. Let me come home to some wins, yeah?"

"Yeah," he agrees. "Let me know the details once they're sorted. I'll handle Coach and Reland."

"Thanks, man," I say, knowing Coach and Scott are going to be understanding of my choice to leave in the middle of the playoffs. Because one, I'm not suiting up again and everyone knows it. And two, they know I'm done for good. For real. It's all over now. "Talk soon." I hang up as Rielle comes to a stop in front of me.

"Where do you keep your passport?" she asks, tapping a navy passport book in her hand.

I frown, because my passport is red. As the dots slowly connect in my hazy head, I widen my eyes at her. "You're coming?"

She stops the tapping and grips her passport book in her fingers tightly. "I don't have to," she rushes to explain.

I laugh, gripping the hem of her shirt and pulling until I can grasp the back of her neck and kiss her mouth. "You'll really come?" I ask the question differently.

I feel her smile against the side of my face. "Of course I

will. But we have to hurry, Torst. We need to be at the airport in an hour and a car is coming for us in thirty minutes. So, tell me all the things you need me to pack."

There's no hesitation in her tone, no uncertainty at all, and the sureness with which she agrees to fly across the Atlantic, meet and say goodbye to the only person who truly matters to me besides her, and step into the lion's den of the Hansen family, fills me with a sense of peace. I breathe in a deep breath and slowly exhale, trying to catch up with all the moving parts.

"Okay." I look up at Rielle. "Here's what we need..." I rattle off a string of clothing we both should pack, inform her where I keep my passport, extra cash, and a small gift I'd like to return to Farmor. When our shared suitcase is packed and our passports, wallets, and phones are in Rielle's purse and my backpack carry-on, she helps me shuffle to the door. My arm is wrapped in a sling and I'm limping but I don't feel the physical pain with my body knotted up in worry for Farmor.

At the last minute, I remind Rielle to grab her camera. She shoots me a strange look, stows it in the carry-on, and laces her fingers with mine.

Then, we head to the airport and board a flight for Oslo.

I'M quiet for the majority of the flight and layover in London. While I'm beyond grateful that Rielle is sitting beside me, with her hand tucked into mine, the closer we draw to my home country, the more my thoughts swirl and my feelings twist.

I'm going to come face-to-face with my father for the first time in years. I'm going to fulfill my promise to Farmor, the one I made decades ago, the one where I put myself out there, accept blame and wrongdoing, and try to make amends. I'm going to do it with Rielle by my side and the fact that she'll witness me cowering before the man who didn't even bother to raise me stings. But I'll swallow my pride and do it because it's the least I can do and the last wish of Farmor's I can fulfill. If making things right with Father brings Farmor peace, then I'll say the words that need to be said with as much sincerity as I can muster.

As the plane descends over Oslo, a lump forms in my throat. No matter where life leads me, coming home always fills me with a rush of emotion. Positive, negative, a combination of the two, there's no denying the lifelong association with the place, the people, and the home that raised me.

I swallow thickly, watching the islands and fjords below grow closer. The snow top mountains are beginning to melt in the warmer May weather. As we descend over the city, my breath catches in my throat and I drink in the beautiful views of my birthplace greedily. After this visit who knows when I'll come back?

Next to me, Rielle squeezes my hand and leans over me, closer to the window. A soft smile touches her lips. "I haven't been here in ages."

Surprise rolls through me. "You've been to Oslo before?"

Wistfulness crosses her expression and she nods. "I've been all over the world. It's all in a past life now."

"With your family?" I dig a little deeper, knowing we're about to land and don't have the necessary amount of time to delve into all of things I want to know about Rielle. But she's not very forthcoming with information about her family and I don't want to let this moment to slip away.

She nods. "Before my mom died."

"Your mom…" I trail off, frowning at her. How did I not know her mother passed? How is she going to handle stepping into a hospital, meeting my farmor on her deathbed? "Rielle," I whisper. "I'm so sorry, sweetheart."

She kisses my shoulder, her eyes sad when they meet mine. "It was a long time ago and still, it feels like yesterday. I'm glad we came, Torst. You need to say goodbye in person."

I wrap my arm around her shoulders, hugging her to my chest. "I don't deserve you, Ri."

"You deserve everything, Torsten."

I kiss the top of her head, holding her, as we touch down in Oslo.

She pulls away and offers a small smile.

"Thank you for coming with me. *Velkommen til Norge, Rielle.*" *Welcome to Norway.*

"I'm just going to exchange dollars for kroners," I tell Torsten as we stand at baggage claim.

I take a step toward the currency exchange but Torsten grabs my wrist and shakes his head.

"You don't need to. I have everything we'll need."

I open my mouth to protest but the look he gives me has me snapping it closed again.

"Don't argue with me about this, Rielle. Please." His voice is sterner than usual too. It's not laced with his usual protective concern but with a hardness that doesn't suit him. I realize that he's shielding himself in impenetrable armor for whatever comes next.

Knowing that he's battling a lot of feelings at the moment, I nod and roll my lips together. Torsten reaches for our suitcase when it circles toward us on the belt. He heaves it off and I can tell that with his sore shoulder and banged-up knee, even lifting the light suitcase cost him. He frowns, grabs the handle, and limps as smoothly as he can toward the exit.

I trail him, noting the small nuances that have shifted in the past twelve hours. He's as gorgeous as ever but his eyes are dimmer, his jawline tighter, his entire persona wrapped in a protective veneer. Is this how I would react to seeing my family again? Is he worried that I'm going to judge him? Or them? Is seeing his grandmother something he needs to do on his own?

"Rielle?" he barks over his shoulder and I scurry to his side, frowning.

Tension rolls off his shoulders and he mutters a swear word as we pass from the terminal into the arrivals hall.

A man approaches Torsten, speaking rapidly in Norwegian. He takes the suitcase from Torsten's hand and gestures toward the parking lot.

I frown up at Torsten, not understanding anything in their exchange.

"That's Lars. He's worked for my family for many years."

"As a..."

"Personal valet."

"To your father?" I guess.

"To me," he murmurs, almost too low for me to hear. "He's been employed in other parts of the household since I moved to America. But when I was a boy..." He lets the sentence drop and I fill in the blanks.

Torsten's family isn't just wealthy. It's more than the Carter kind of wealth I grew up around. His family has a history, deep roots that stretch back to a time period when children had personal valets. The realization hits me hard as a thousand little things snap into place. The ease with which Torsten paid off my Jerry Jensen loan. The way he laughed at me wanting to pitch in for rent even though the idea was asinine. The fact that he gave me full use of his SUV and shrugged that he can always buy another. I knew he had money but this is more than money. This is the level above *money*.

I'm escorted to a white BMW and Lars holds the door open for me without making eye contact. I slide into the back seat, surprised when Torsten maneuvers in beside me instead of riding up front where he would be more comfortable.

"Torsten," I whisper as Lars closes the trunk. "What exactly does your family do?"

"We socialize. We marry well. We keep up appearances. And we have a family business, oil, that could grow for at least two more generations with little involvement, but we all fight over it like vultures who may not live to see another day."

My head spins as I process his words, as I note the angry glint in his eyes.

"So your family is…aristocracy?" I ask hesitantly.

"My family are a bunch of assholes," he clarifies.

In the driver's seat, Lars's shoulders stiffen. But he pulls out of the parking lot without a word.

THE HOSPITAL HALLWAY smells like antiseptic and hard soap. It brings back a slew of memories I've done my best to forget.

Mom's final days. Images of her bald head, her drawn face, cheeks hollow and sunken, flicker through my mind. The feel of her hand, her bones frail, her skin nearly translucent, tugs on my memories.

I bite the corner of my mouth until the prick of pain eases the throb in my chest.

Torsten gives me an empathetic look. "You holding up okay? I wish I knew sooner, sweetheart. You don't have to stay. Lars can—"

"I'll wait out here," I cut him off.

His gaze searches mine for one more beat before he nods curtly, takes the backpack we used as a carry-on from my hands, and steps into the hospital room.

I plop down on a bench in the hallway, letting the random

chatter from the nearby nurse's station roll over me, even though I don't understand any of it. I'm staring into space, trying to compartmentalize the unexpected zing of emotions, of memories and moments I thought I'd moved on from, when a shadow falls over me.

I look up into the pale, icy blue gaze of a man who looks too similar to Torsten to not be a relation.

"Hi," I manage, scooting down on the bench in case the newcomer wants to sit.

After a moment, he does. His expression is curious, his eyes narrowed. He doesn't look friendly or menacing but he gives off a vibe that has my nerves snapping to attention.

"You are American."

"Yes."

"You came with Torsten." He inquires with statements, as if everything he says is a fact. It's unnerving but since it's also true, I nod.

"And you are?" I lift an eyebrow.

"Your brother-in-law." His face remains impassive, his façade even thicker than the one Torsten wrapped himself in when we landed.

I don't know how much Torsten's family knows of our marriage so I keep my face blank as I hold out a hand. "It's nice to meet you. I'm Rielle."

"I know." He shakes my hand, his touch impersonal, like he shakes hands for a living.

"I'm sorry about your farmor." I tip my head to the hospital room that Torsten entered.

He swallows and averts his gaze, mumbling a word in Norwegian that I think means "thank you."

"Far! Far!" A little boy turns the corner of the hallway and barrels toward us. His blue eyes are sparkling and his blond hair is almost white. He slides to a stop in front of the man beside me and I realize this little boy, with the bright smile and glittering eyes, is Torsten's nephew.

Why didn't he tell me he has a brother? A nephew?

Like you told him about your niece?

Torsten and I have steered clear of talking about our families. Is it because we both know how painful it is? Or is it deeper than that?

I flick the thought out of my head and turn my attention to the enthusiastic, little boy.

His father speaks to him in Norwegian and his shoulders dip, his expression growing serious. A moment later, an out-of-breath woman appears at the end of the hallway, a shock of fear blooming in her expression when she sees the little boy and his father. What are their names?

Torsten's brother stands and strides toward the woman. His voice is quiet but his words are clipped as he gestures to the boy.

The boy glances up at me shyly.

I smile at him and stick out my hand. Not wanting to create any additional family drama, I say, "Hey there. My name is Rielle."

He places his small hand in mine and shakes with a lot more warmth than his dad. "I'm Magnus," he responds in perfect English.

"It's a pleasure to meet you."

"You too. Do you like dinosaurs?" he asks innocently, pulling two small dinosaur figures from his pocket.

I study the bright orange and green toys. "Is that a T-Rex and a brachiosaurus you've got there?"

His eyes light up, the deepest blue of all the men I've met in his family, and he nods eagerly.

I place a hand to my chest and gasp in mock surprise. "How'd you sneak them into the hospital?"

He giggles, delighted that I'm playing along. "I had to hide them in my pocket."

"You're lucky they haven't grown to full size yet or they might not fit in the hallway."

He laughs again.

"How old are you?" I ask.

He holds up four fingers. "How old are you?"

"I don't have enough fingers to show you. I'm twenty-four."

His eyes widen as if I told him I'm four hundred. I laugh.

"You smell pretty," he says simply, blinking long lashes at me.

"Thank you, Magnus. I just got off a very long airplane ride, with a stopover in London. So I'm glad to hear I don't stink like rotten eggs."

He tips his head back, exposing his neck, as he giggles again. I grin, loving how affectionate and sweet he is. "Where did you come from?" he asks when his laughter subsides.

"America."

His eyes widen. "I have an uncle who—"

The door to Farmor's hospital room opens as said uncle steps into the hallway. Magnus stops talking as his mouth hangs open in surprise, his eyes wide as he takes in the hulking stature of his uncle.

Torsten's brother's eyes snap to us, then to Torsten, and his back straightens. He crosses his arms over his chest and glares at his brother. The older woman, who I surmise is Magnus's nanny, wrings her hands nervously and brushes hair out of her eyes.

Magnus breaks the tension by exclaiming, "It's really you!"

Torsten's head whips to the little boy who's nearly bouncing on his toes in excitement.

"You're really a hockey player!" Magnus rushes him and throws his arms around Torsten's legs.

Torsten's brother frowns and steps forward, reaching out to grab his son's arm. Before he can, Torsten wraps an arm around the boy's shoulders protectively. "What's your name, little man?"

"Magnus." Magnus beams up at Torsten as Torsten bends down to his eye level. "I'm your biggest fan and you're my uncle."

Torsten's face twists as he glares at his brother over Magnus's head. His brother has the good sense to look ashamed and drops his gaze to the ground. He says something in Norwegian and Torsten nods.

Torsten pulls his nephew close again and Magus practically vibrates with excitement. He grins at me and I wink back. Torsten catches the exchange and his expression softens. He whispers something to Magnus who goes to stand by his father as Torsten takes two strides toward me. I notice he's hiding his limp well even though his arm is still wrapped in a sling.

"How'd it go?" I whisper as he sits on the bench.

"She wants to see you," he whispers back nervously.

"Me?" I press my hand to my chest.

Torsten nods. "I know it's a lot to ask. But will you…" He trails off, an apology on the tip of his tongue.

Before he can finish his question, I nod. "Of course."

He clears his throat. "I'm going to, um, I'll just grab a coffee with my brother. I'll be back in ten minutes tops. I…I'm sorry I brought you here, Rielle," he whispers, brushing a chaste kiss to the crown of my head.

His words scrape across my soul, cutting deeper than I ever imagined. I shouldn't have come. Months ago, Torsten admitted he didn't want me to meet his family, that he'd only bring me to Oslo to fulfill his farmor's request. But haven't things changed? Haven't we grown since then?

The realization that he still feels the same way slams into me. Have I read more into our relationship than he has?

Just hours ago, we had sex and I fell asleep in his arms. I felt cherished and desired. Wanted and safe. Now, I just feel naïve. The depths of my feelings for him rock through me because suddenly, I'm battling tears.

I watch Torsten's back recede down the hallway. His shoulders are stiff as he nods at whatever his brother says to him. He never turns around but at the last minute, Magnus does, and the little boy frowns at whatever he reads in my expression.

Once they're gone, I rub my hands under my eyes, pinch my cheeks for some color, and try to muss up the roots of my hair for a little volume. I can't even imagine how horrid I must look after a fifteen-hour journey, running on minimal sleep, too much caffeine, and a dash of heartache. I blow out a deep breath and stand from the bench. I hate that I'm going to cross the threshold to Farmor's—when did I start calling her that?—hospital room and pretend that her grandson and I married for love. Especially now, when my feelings for him seem unreciprocated.

CHAPTER EIGHTEEN
RIELLE

I step into the dimly lit room and the memories of years ago, when my brother and I stood at our mother's bedside and whispered our goodbyes, rocks through me. The memories flip through my mind quickly and scatter, violently, like shrapnel.

"Rielle?" a voice calls from the bed. Her voice is thin, reedy, floating on top of the air like an ocean breeze. It's fleeting, here now, gone in how many hours? Her accent is thick, wrapping around my name like a hug I wish I could fall into.

I step closer to her bedside and tuck my hair behind my ears. "Hi, Farmor," I whisper, using Torsten's name for her.

She manages a tiny smile of acknowledgement. "I hoped you would come."

"It's a pleasure to meet you," I say.

"I wish we had more time. I'd like to know you."

"Me too."

"Do you love him?" she asks, her eyes suddenly sharp, searching mine with a ferocity to uncover any deceit.

My heart swells into my throat as tears fill my eyes. The relief that I won't have to lie to her face on her deathbed fills me with as much relief as the truth does when it bursts from my lips on a sob. "Yes."

The corners of her mouth lift and she covers my hand, the one clutching the railing of her bedside like a lifeline, with hers. "Then why do you cry?"

"Because," I stammer, my head whirling as the truth, the past, the now all collide in a burst of light that nearly blinds me. "Because I want him to love me back."

"Oh, my dear," she breathes out. A flare of amusement sparks in her eyes, so much like Torsten's, and for a moment, I see her the way he must have. Full of life and light and energy. Giving of love and understanding and empathy.

A tear spills over onto my cheek and slides down around my chin. I brush it away with the back of my hand, embarrassed that in this woman's final days, I'm the one seeking comfort. The ache that's wrapped around my heart since my mother passed squeezes, piercing me with an agonizing pain. Every day since she passed, I've missed her fiercely. As I've grown older, I've wished for a mother figure to reach out to, to look to for advice. Claire's mom, Mary, has been the closest female role model I've had since Mom but this brief exchange with Farmor leads me to believe she would have gladly stepped into the role.

"I know you and my grandson didn't marry for love."

Shock zaps through my body and my mouth drops open.

She laughs lightly at the horror that washes over my face. I'm too slow to conceal it and honestly, right now, I don't want to. I want this kind woman with compassionate eyes to tell me what to do. To help me make sense of this complicated mess I've made with Torsten. Have I fallen so completely in love with my husband that I can't even hide it from his nearly ninety-year-old grandma? Am I that transparent? Does Torsten know? Doesn't *he* see it?

She pats my hand again and offers a knowing look. "My grandson has been gone a long time but I still know him. And it brings me great joy to know the truth."

My brows lift so high, I imagine them in my hairline. "Farmor, I…we—"

She squeezes my hand. "I know, Rielle." She lifts her hand slowly and points to a box on her bedside table. "Hand me that box."

I pick it up and place it in her hand.

"Help me open it," she says, her hand shaking as her strength wanes.

I pull open the top of the jewelry box and gasp at the ring inside. It's a stunning, deep blue sapphire in a marquise setting in a band of small blue diamonds. My mother used to wear a blue diamond pendant necklace that was given to her by her father on her wedding day. It was her something blue and I used to look at it longingly as a little girl. I always imagined I'd wear it on my own wedding day, until the night I left and tried my best to erase my entire life up until that point from my thoughts. It makes me smile to realize that my something blue was hydrangeas in my hair. And yet, I know for a fact that my fake wedding day to Torsten was just as happy an occasion as my mother's real wedding day to my father. I take comfort in knowing that Mom would adore Torsten.

"It's yours," Farmor whispers, her voice bringing me back to the present.

"What?" I frown, wondering if she's slipped into another memory like I just did.

But her eyes are clear when they meet mine. "I gave this to Torsten a long time ago. For him to give to his future bride. He brought it back to me tonight to ask my permission for you to have it. Oh, I can't believe he hasn't already put it on your finger, my dear. But I want you to have the ring. To wear it. For you are a Hansen, even if it took you longer to realize it." She plucks the ring from the box and drops it in my palm, closing my fingers around the stone and holding my hand in hers.

"Promise me something?" She rests back against her pillows.

"Anything," I say, still trying to process the part where she placed an incredibly rare, expensive ring in my hand like I somehow deserve it. This is the small box Torsten stashed in the carry-on. Does Torsten truly want me to wear it? Did he really bring it here for his farmor's blessing? Or does he want her to believe he's happy and secure so she can pass without worrying about him?

My conflicting thoughts are too painful to consider at the moment. Instead, I swallow thickly and give my attention to Farmor's request.

"Make sure he makes things right with his father. He needs the closure to move on and choose happiness. It will take some time. He will resist it. He may even shut you out. But don't give up on him. Torsten is a stubborn man, a lot more like my son than he thinks he is. The men in this family take too long to see what is right in front of their faces but in the end, they always wake up."

I nod at her words, not understanding the full meaning behind them, but grasping that it's important to her that Torsten and his father make amends. "I will," I promise, intending to keep it.

"Don't give up on him," she mutters again as her eyelids grow heavy. "Will you sit with me? I'm so tired."

"It's okay," I tell her, wrapping my fingers with hers so the stone rests between our palms. "I'm here. I'll stay. You rest."

Her eyes flutter closed and for a blink, I'm ten years old, watching my mother slip away in front of my eyes.

I don't know how long I sit at Farmor's bedside.

At some point, the door swings open and Torsten and his brother shadow the entrance. Their hulking frames seem to invade the space, the angry slashes of their mouths, the sharp angles of their cheekbones, the concern blazing in their matching eyes sucks the oxygen from the room.

They take me in, sitting at Farmor's bedside and holding her hand as if she was mine instead of theirs. Torsten's brother's expression softens and he looks at me like he's seeing me for the first time.

But anguish streaks across Torsten's face. His mouth twists, his eyes burn, and he turns away as if I've hurt him. As if my presence fills him with shame.

WE'RE quiet when we leave the hospital. The tension between us is thicker than I've ever felt it. What shifted? What happened with his brother? Why is he upset that I visited with Farmor after he asked me to?

Anguish and despair roll off of Torsten in surges that threaten to drown me. I feel his disappointment in my throat. I carry his hurt in my stomach. I can barely look at him for how much it seems to destroy him when his eyes meet mine.

Lars drives us through the city streets and I pretend to gaze out the window with interest, as if I'm taking in all the sights of Oslo. In reality, I don't see anything but a blur. I assume we're going to a hotel, but we stop in front of a mansion on the outskirts of the city that has anxiety crawling through my veins like fire ants.

Lars opens the door for me and I stumble out, catching myself at the last moment by grasping the door. Lars glares down his nose at me. In perfect English, he says, "Welcome to Hansen Manor."

"Thank you," I sputter, clearing my throat. I follow Lars up the steps to a huge wooden door that swings open before we reach it.

Staff members bustle about inside as Lars leads me into a

foyer that rivals the one in my childhood home, with a sweeping staircase and blinding crystal chandelier.

The back of my neck tingles and I know Torsten has entered the home and is standing behind me. More than anything, I want to turn, wrap my arms around his hips, and bury my face in his chest. I want to feel his fingers in my hair, let his warmth seep into my chilled skin, let the sound of his heartbeat slow the racing of mine. I want to know that we're okay.

Instead, I shuffle back a step. Torsten wraps his arm around my shoulders, guiding me forward. His touch is hesitant, as if he doesn't know how to act around me now that we're in his childhood home. The wall he seems to erect between us is confusing and hurtful. I try to lean into his touch but he straightens, his arm slipping away as his fingers press into the small of my back.

I smile politely at the staff as Lars leads us to a room. Torsten shuffles along slowly and I know from his breathing that his leg and shoulder are causing him pain, to say nothing of the concussion he's battling. He needs rest and care. The last thing I should do is pile more stress on his already over-flowing plate. So I bite back my questions, swallow down my hurt, and vow to do what is in his best interest.

Once we cross the threshold into our room, Lars closes the door behind us. Our room is more than just a room, it's like a hotel suite, with a sitting area, a desk, an en-suite bathroom, and I wager, a closet larger than my old apartment in Southie.

"Rielle."

I look at him, searching his eyes for something to latch onto, some emotion to help me feel closer to him and not like we're on opposite sides of the Atlantic, about to sink.

"Say something," he demands. "The first thing that comes to mind."

I hold back all of my questions about us, forcing myself to

bury my fears regarding our relationship. Instead, I think of Farmor and her request. "Make things right with your dad."

Torsten jerks back as if I slapped him. A shudder drops over his eyes and I realize too late that he was trying to connect with me too and I ruined it.

"Torsten, wait—" I reach for him.

But he holds up an arm and turns his back, gesturing that he needs to use the bathroom. I watch him limp across the room with apologies dying on my tongue and tears filling my eyes.

I hate myself for involving Rielle in all of my family drama. Over a month ago, she warned me she didn't want to lie to a sweet, old lady's face and that's exactly what I made her do. On Farmor's deathbed no less.

The anguish in Rielle's face haunts me. The hurt in her eyes lances at my chest, cutting me wide open. The way she looked at me and told me to make things right with my father, like I'm some spoiled, overindulgent child, landed like a jab to the jaw.

I can barely look at her without disgust and shame for myself welling in my throat, clogging my ability to breathe.

Early this morning, I went to the hospital to sit with Farmor. She'd already slipped into unconsciousness but the rise and fall of her chest soothed me. Just knowing she was still here calmed some of the erratic thoughts fighting for room in my mind. After an hour, I kissed her forehead, thanked her for giving me a beautiful childhood, for believing in me when no one else did, and blessed her spirit. I slipped from her room, casting one last look over my shoulder. But Farmor asleep in a hospital bed isn't how I want to remember the woman with mischievous eyes and a too-big heart. When I arrived back at the house, Rielle was still asleep.

Now, I'm dressing to meet with my father and Anders. We're sitting down with my uncle Erik and his sons, Daniel and Johan. The lawyers are meeting us to go over Farmor's wishes, things related to the business and the future, things that can be discussed given the current situation. More than anything, I want to race back to the hospital and be at Farmor's side but Father demanded I attend this meeting and since I promised Farmor last night that I'd make nice during my time here, I've agreed.

The bathroom door opens and Rielle steps out. God, she's beautiful. Her hair is a wild curtain of curls. It's different than the sleek, straight style she rocked when she worked at Hendrix. She's clad in jeans and a light sweater, casual boots on her feet.

I clear my throat. "I'm speaking with my father this morning."

She gives me a genuine smile. "Good."

"There's horses if you ride?"

She shrugs. "On occasion."

It strikes me just how little I know about her life, her past, her. It leaves me feeling more unsettled, more disjointed. I've brought Rielle to Oslo, to my family home, to meet my farmor as she passes into the next life and I don't even know if she rides horses or where her family lives now or if she likes her meat cooked well done or medium. Another layer of shame settles in my chest, this one nearly reaching the base of my throat.

I run my hand over my head. "What are you going to do this morning?"

She picks up the DSLR camera I gave her and places the strap around her neck. "Explore."

I frown. "It's not safe to just wander—"

"Magnus is coming with me."

The sight of my nephew, of Anders' son, running toward me flares in my mind. Of course I knew I had a nephew but

God, is he already four? Did I really miss his entire life, never once meeting him? My disgust with myself grows larger. Soon, it will eat me entirely. That is, if I don't suffocate from it first.

"Don't worry about me. I can entertain myself." Rielle moves to pass me but at the last moment, I catch her wrist. The flash of blue catches my eye as I hold her tightly, my gaze drawn to the sapphire and diamond ring on her index finger.

"She gave it to you," I murmur, shock racing through me. I promised Farmor, in addition to making things right with my father, that I'd give my future wife, the woman who owns my heart, her ring. I brought it back, hoping we could talk about it today, hoping I'd have some time with Farmor to explain that my relationship is complicated but not without deep feelings. At least, on my end. And yet, Farmor already knows because she gave Rielle her ring.

Rielle stiffens beside me. "Do you not want me to wear it? It's just, while we're here, after everything your farmor and I shared..." She shrugs and uses her other hand to twist the ring off her finger. She holds it out to me. "Forget it. Here."

I back away from the ring as if it will burn me. In many ways, taking it from Rielle would. "No. Wear it. I want you to."

She studies me for a long moment before sighing. Then, she jams the ring on her finger and walks toward the door. When her hand touches the knob, she turns and looks at me over her shoulder. Her eyes swim with hurt and shine with sincerity. "Good luck today, Torsten. I'm rooting for you."

Then, she's gone and with her, the resolve I've been clinging to, to keep it all together, slips.

I lower myself to the edge of the mattress and try to get my head on straight. The room spins, making me nauseous.

Farmor is dying. Rielle is wearing her ring. Magnus called me uncle. I still have to fulfill my promise.

Exhaustion sweeps through me, making my limbs heavy,

my movements sluggish. My shoulder feels less sore today but my knee throbs from not resting it. Lingering effects of my concussion float on the periphery of my vision. The play-offs, the game, the hit all seem like they happened eons ago. Has it really only been two days?

I rub sleep from my eyes as a sharp knock sounds on my door.

"Come in," I say in Norwegian.

Lars pops his head around the door. "It's time. They're waiting for you, Master Torsten."

I sigh and pull myself up. It's time to face the music. It's time to come and do the thing I promised I'd do.

In many ways, my time is up and simultaneously, just starting.

I pull a sweater on over my button-up shirt and give myself a quick glance in the mirror. No matter how I look, Father will have a derisive comment tucked away. Blowing out a breath, I step toward the door.

As I pass Lars, I remind him for the umpteenth time, "It's just Torsten."

As always, he doesn't respond.

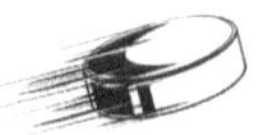

I WALK through the dark mahogany hallways of my father's house and a million memories of my childhood ripple over my skin. Like skipping stones, some skirt the surface of my consciousness, not requiring additional consideration. Others cause ripples in my mind, stirring up past mistakes and scabbed-over wounds. And still others sink deep, piercing my soul.

Father's disappointment in me is well-known and well-documented. Anyone who worked in the Hansen employ over the past twenty-something years can recall the tension between us, even an ocean apart. But Father is Farmor's son and I love Farmor so here I am. I take a deep inhale and force myself to stand as straight as my sore shoulder and bum knee will allow. Right before I push inside Father's office, where we're meeting, Anders enters the hallway. He lets out a low whistle and I can't stop the grin that splits my face.

It's a thing we did as kids, when on the lookout for Father. After our mother left us, Father spent the following year in a fog, oscillating between periods of darkness and depression and anger and rage. On the nights we knew better than to cross his path, Anders and I would whistle a low, three-note melody, similar to the Common Rosefinch which could be found in these parts.

I glance up at him as he strides toward me, his hands in his pockets, a boyish expression on his face.

"My son is enamored with your wife," he says, with more warmth in his tone than yesterday.

"She's pretty easy to fall for," I agree.

He looks me over and nods. Lifting a hand to his face, he scrapes it along his jawline the same way I do when I'm in uncharted territory, uncertain how to proceed. "Listen, brother," he begins in our native tongue, "I love Farmor just as much as you."

"I know that."

He rocks back on his heels, stuffing his hands back into his pockets. "I'm tired of holding a grudge for reasons I no longer care about. It's been too long."

I frown. "What do you mean? The reasons are clear. I left the family fold, I turned my back on the Hansen name, I didn't step up the way I was supposed to and instead, booked it to America." I tick off the reasons on my fingers. What else have I done for my family to despise me so much?

Apparently something because surprise washes over my

brother's expression. "That's what you think?" he asks in a low voice.

"What?" I narrow my eyes at him, trying to connect dots that aren't lining up. "What else have I done?"

"You mean, you didn't skim money from the business to pay for hockey? For the ice time and the uniforms and the travel?"

My blood turns cold as ice spreads through my veins. My chest nearly caves in on itself as I stare into my brother's eyes and realize he truly believes the accusations he's leveling me with.

"Skim money?" I hiss, the muscle in my jaw ticking frantically. "Steal from my own family? Steal when we all know there was enough money to pay for my hockey?"

"Shh," Anders says, a warning in his eyes. He grabs me by the arm and pulls me around the corner, away from Father's office door. "I thought that's what, that's what Father and Uncle Erik told me."

I drop my head back and let out a chuckle that sounds more like a growl. "I can't fucking believe it. All this time, I thought I, I thought you felt like I abandoned you guys, chose hockey over our family, over our stupidly privileged lives."

When I meet Anders' eyes again, he shakes his head. "No. Never. I was always proud of you for hockey. Why do you think my son knows all of your stats? Not that Father knows that but..." He trails off and sighs. "I'm sorry, Torsten. Truly. I wish I reached out to you years ago. When you first left and Father told me about the skimming, I was too angry to reach out. Furious really. By the time my anger simmered, I'd been working with Father and Uncle Erik for a couple of years and by then, honestly, I resented you for leaving. I hated that you got away, out from under all of this..." He tosses his arms wide and I wince at the hurt in his tone. "Then I met Elin and my life shifted. I was too wrapped up in her, in our future, to go digging into the past." He shrugs. "I let too many years go by."

I shake my head. "Nah, Anders. It's not all on you, man. I could have picked up the phone too and I didn't."

"After Elin left—"

"Left?"

Anders' shoulders dip. "She took off on us about a year and half ago. Said it was too much. The family drama, the constant posturing and positioning among father's generation. Daniel and Johan aren't like that. They're like me. Us." He taps me in the chest with the back of his hand. "It was too much for her."

"Shit, I'm sorry, Anders. I didn't know. Farmor never said a word." I frown. Why didn't Farmor tell me? *Why didn't you ever ask?*

"It's fine. I have Magnus and he's"—he grins suddenly, a little sheepishly—"he's my world."

"He's pretty incredible," I agree.

Anders glances in the direction of Father's office. "Let's go in there and lay it all out, Torsten. You don't want this life, you never have."

"True," I agree, frowning at him. "What do you have in mind?"

"I don't want this life either. Not the way Father runs thing. Constant manipulation and pitting family member against family member. Plotting and scheming, creating dramas. You think I want this to be my legacy? What I leave for Magnus?"

I narrow my eyes, seeing my brother through a new lens. "Fatherhood's changed you, Anders."

He shrugs. "You think it won't but trust me, it will change you too."

"Nah, Rielle and I, we're not—"

He chuckles and clasps my shoulder. "Trust me, you are.

You just don't know it yet. Come on, we better get going. You with me?"

I whistle back our three-note code and Anders grins.

Mixed feelings tinged with nostalgia wrap around me as I follow my brother toward Father's office. Decades of hurt and anger and tension could have been avoided. If Anders is telling the truth and I strongly suspect he is, then Father concocted one hell of a story to get my family to despise me. But why would he do that? What is he after?

Anders storms into Father's office like he owns it and I jump when the door slams into the wall, another childhood memory rolling over me. But back then, Father was the only one throwing open doors.

Everyone is already seated around the conference table and look up in alarm. My cousins, Johan and Daniel, wear confused expressions. Uncle Erik looks irritated. The lawyers appear surprised. And Father, well, he sneers at me and lifts his chin. "So the prodigal son returns."

"Nice of you to greet me when I arrived," I mutter, walking to the table.

He narrows his eyes. "What's wrong with your leg?"

"Took a tough hit." I lower myself into a vacant chair and Anders slides into the one beside me.

Father shrugs. "That will happen when you choose to work with your back instead of your brain."

Anders glowers at Father.

I grin at the table. "The prodigal son, huh? An interesting comparison when you consider that I made my own fortune from my own skill, talents, and didn't need to piggyback off the family name."

Johan opens his mouth but Anders cuts him off before he can speak.

"You lied to us." He points at Father.

Father frowns, gesturing with his hand for Anders to hurry up and say whatever he wants to say.

"Torsten never skimmed any money. He never stole from the business. He never did anything except follow his dream and have you badmouth his name, smear his reputation in Norway. You made our family turn our backs on him and let him believe it was his fault." Anders' voice shakes at the end. I sit up straighter in my chair, stunned at the length my brother is going through to right this wrong.

It dawns on me that Anders truly had no idea and is remorseful for all the time we lost. At one point in time, he was my best friend. My big brother. He protected me and right now, he's doing it again.

Johan glances at me. "Is this true?"

Father sighs and glances at one of the lawyers who flips open his portfolio, signaling it's time to begin.

"Hang on." Daniel holds out a hand, and lifts his chin at Father. "Is it true?"

"Every word," I respond.

The atmosphere in the room drops several degrees as a thin layer of ice spreads throughout the room.

Johan turns to his father. "Did you know?"

"The *truth*," Daniel demands.

One of the lawyer's phone rings and he excuses himself to take the call.

Father sighs and glances at the ceiling, as if the universe owes him something other than a swift jab to the jaw.

Uncle Erik clears his throat and nods.

Johan mutters a string of curse words as Daniel cuts me a look filled with apology.

"How could—" Father begins to berate his brother but the lawyer slips back into the room, his expression somber.

And I know. I know it in my bones that Farmor has passed. I feel it like a tidal wave pulling me down to the depths of the sea. My hands clench into fists and a coldness sweeps through my limbs, causing my chest to ache and my eyes to burn.

"Greta has passed," the lawyer whispers. He looks traumatized at having to be the one to share this news.

My father bows his head for a long moment before raising it. "She was a good woman."

"She was more than that," Anders snaps.

Father extends a hand to the lawyers. "Shall we begin?"

Johan scoffs. He mutters something about our whole family being fucked up.

In this moment, stunned but not shocked, I wholeheartedly agree.

How are we supposed to talk about business now? How could Father discuss anything other than how special, how important Farmor was to all of us? To this family? My hands shake as I repeat the lawyer's words in my mind. She's gone. I swallow back the bile climbing the walls of my throat and focus on my breathing which feels too shallow. Floaters swim in my peripheral vision and my stomach churns.

The lawyer's voice begins to read aloud and then Father slams the top of the table, Uncle Erik swears, and the room grows eerily quiet.

"Torsten?" Anders shakes my shoulder.

I glance up, meeting his eyes, so familiar to my own. "What is it? What's wrong?"

He gives me a look of disbelief. "Farmor left the company, all of its shares, to the four of us." He gestures to me and our cousins.

Johan looks dumbfounded and Daniel's mouth is wide open.

"What?" I ask, confusion rocking through me.

"Daniel, Johan, and I each inherited twenty-four percent of the company. She's left the other twenty-eight percent to you. You are the majority shareholder. The majority of the company is now in your name."

My vision clouds over and I grip the armrests, knowing I'm about to pass out.

Right before I do, Anders wraps his arm around me in a one-armed hug and I cling to reality even as the Earth shifts under my feet.

"Welcome back, brother. I've really missed you."

I nod but it's not his voice that echoes in my mind.

It's Father's. "I'm contesting this. She can't have meant to leave Torsten in charge, especially not now that he's married to a woman he barely knows. A woman who will take half when he fails at marriage the same way he's failed at everything else."

T he moment I see Torsten's face, I know something is wrong.

I rush to him, my hands hesitant as they grasp his. He's cold to the touch, his eyes void, his expression blank.

"What's wrong?" I ask.

"What's right?" he responds and I recall that night at Taps, over two months ago now.

I frown and lead Torsten to the sitting area of our bedroom. We both sink to the couch, our knees touching.

"Torsten? Talk to me."

"Farmor died," he murmurs.

My hands clench his as a wave of emotion I didn't expect to feel rolls through me. "I'm so sorry." I shift closer and wrap my arms around him. "I'm so sorry, baby. I'm glad I got to meet her, even for a moment. Thank you for bringing me."

Confusion ripples over his face as he stares at me. "You really *wanted* to come?"

"I wanted to be with you. Be here for you," I stammer.

"Why?" he asks and it's as if he's looking at me for the first time. There's a cold dejectedness in his expression that alarms me.

"Because you're my husband," I say slowly.

"Am I? Farmor's gone now. We don't need to keep up this charade." He disentangles our hands and jumps to his feet.

He paces back and forth in front of me, like a caged beast desperate to break free. A memory, a moment when I once paced in front of him, worried and hopeful and overwhelmed, blooms in my mind but I blink it away.

"What are you saying? Torsten?"

The longer he paces without answering me, the more my nerves ricochet through my body, the more my anxiety unfurls in my limbs. It feels like one of Magnus's dinosaurs took up residence in my chest and I press the heel of my hand into my breastbone to loosen the pressure building there.

He stops suddenly and turns toward me. His blue eyes gleam with a million things I don't understand except for one. Acceptance. Whatever he's about to say, he's already accepted. He's made his peace with it. And it's going to decimate me.

I brace for the impact as his lips part. "We jumped into this. We jumped into everything because I wanted to stay in the US and you were struggling under your loan payments. But now…things have changed. We don't have to stay in a situation we never would have found ourselves in otherwise." He shakes his head before meeting my gaze again. His eyes are wild. "We should get divorced."

I squint up at him. "What? Why?" I shake my head. "You're not making any sense."

"I'm making plenty of sense." He crosses his arms over his chest. "My farmor has passed. I've inherited the majority of the company."

I suck in a breath, not expecting that at all.

"My career is finished. My body is fucking breaking. What am I going to do in the US anyway?"

"What?" I jump to my feet now, my hurt bleeding into anger. Anger is good; I know what to do with anger. "Wasn't that the whole point of this?" I gesture between us. "For you to stay in the States?"

He nods, his eyes bleeding with emotion but then he blinks and it's as if triage managed to stem the flow. "Yes, it was. Because I didn't know what was waiting for me here. My brother and I, my cousins, we've made amends. I have a nephew, Ri. A kid I could adore. This is my childhood home. My family." His voice holds a tone of longing and it rips through me.

He wants his home.

Haven't I felt that way before? When I was missing Mom? When I was desperate for Dad to really see me? But when I left, I swore I'd never return. Until now, my pride has always prevented me from trying to find a way back. Isn't it fortunate for Torsten that his family is welcoming him with open arms again?

My throat expands and suddenly, breathing is difficult. Panic rises in my chest, my fingers tingle, and dread fills my limbs with dead weight. I suck air into my lungs but it's too thin and I can't catch it. Can't hang onto it long enough.

"Rielle?" Torsten strides forward and lowers me to the couch.

He's breaking up with me. He promised if I was his, he'd never let me go. But now…

He's *divorcing* me.

Oh God. I bend over as Torsten guides my head between my knees.

"Breathe, Ri. I got you. You're okay." His words are meant to soothe but they don't. Because he's leaving.

Or, wait a minute, *I'm* the one leaving?

How could I have been so stupid? How could I have trusted him? I know better than to let people in. I knew this would happen eventually and yet…

I can't bring myself to regret it either because for the first time since my mom died, I felt like I had a real home. And it felt good.

That loss slams into me and I grip the material of my jeans over my knees, searching for the air that won't come.

"Rielle? Ri, come on, baby. You're scaring me." Torsten's voice holds a thread of panic.

His terror allows me to grasp onto the moment, to cling to it. I catch the air and suck it in, hold it in my chest as my heart feels ready to explode.

"Rielle." Torsten strokes his fingers through my hair. He murmurs nonsensical things that I can't focus on because my mind is already going a mile a minute. My thoughts are leapfrogging over each other with the fastest way to extricate myself from this situation. Fight or flight and right now, I'm desperate to flee.

I need to go home.

Oh God. I don't even have a home.

My hands shake and a buzzing sound whirs around my head, like a fly I can't catch.

"Rielle, talk to me. I didn't mean to spring this on you. I thought you'd be happy, relieved."

"Relieved?" I manage to sputter, my voice several octaves too high. I swallow and dip my head, tucking my hair behind my ears. I stand on shaky legs and put some distance between us. My panic attack recedes but still clings to the edges of my mind. "You thought I'd be re-relieved to know that you want to divorce me? That you want to put me on a plane back, back to B-Boston. Without you?" Tears stream down my cheeks.

Torsten stares at me in horror. He stands and I shake my head, stepping away from him.

Anguish twists his expression and his eyes hold mine, pleading. For what? "This isn't the life you want, Ri. You want a fulfilling career. You want kids. You want a future with a man you're going to build it with, brick by brick by brick."

I point at him accusingly. "How the hell do you know what I want? Have you ever asked me? Have you bothered to find out? Or did you just assume that you—the older, wiser, more experienced, and financially sound Torsten Hansen knows best?"

He sighs and rakes a hand through his hair. His eyes grow shiny for all the wrong reasons as he reaches for me again.

"You want a divorce? Fine, I'll give you a divorce. I'll be on the next flight to the States too so I won't be in your hair any longer." I turn toward the suitcase, almost screaming when I remember that we shared one. "I'm taking the suit-case." I shout at his still form.

I pack angrily, throwing my things into the suitcase.

Torsten remains quiet, watching me with distrusting eyes. "Rielle," he murmurs as I zip up the bag.

I stand up and cross my arms around my stomach, as if physically holding myself together like Scotch tape. "What?"

"You don't have to—I don't want you to…" He trails off.

"Say what you want. Don't think about it, just say it," I tell him.

"I want what's best for you," he responds automatically, his voice breaking.

And dammit, I can tell he means it. His sincerity makes everything hurting inside of me ache even more. He's dismantling me, one word and desperate glance at a time. He broke through all the walls I built and now he's knocking over the foundation so I'll have nothing solid to start over on.

I feel myself retreating inside, looking for a shield, a way to fend off the giant, gaping hole Torsten Hansen is leaving me with.

But it's no use.

Because I'm in love with my husband and—

"And I'm not it," he whispers, his eyes shuddering closed.

I slip into autopilot, my body locking down. I just have to make it to the plane. Then, in front of several hundred strangers, I can break down and sob my eyes out. But not now, not in front of Torsten.

I can't handle any more humiliation right now. I turn my back to him and pull my cell phone out of my pocket. The tiniest, so small it barely exists, flicker of relief occurs when I realize there's a flight in three hours to New York. I just need to get on it and then I can figure it out from there.

I clear my throat. "I'm going to ask Lars if he'll take me to the airport."

"Rielle, wait a second." Torsten reaches for my arm but I shuffle back, avoiding his touch. If he touches me, I'll crumble. And it isn't time for that yet.

"Send me the divorce papers and I'll sign. I'll text you the address I end up at."

He frowns, concern flaring in his eyes. He looks miserable and if it was any moment but this one, I'd wrap my arms around him. But I can't. Right now, I need to look out for myself because obviously, no one else is. "What do you mean? The address you end up at? Go back home." He winces. "Go to the penthouse."

I shake my head and twist his grandmother's ring from my finger. I place it on the nightstand and dig into my purse for his gold credit card. When I pull it from my wallet, he swears. His hand snakes out and curls over mine. "Put that back," he demands.

"No thank you," I say cordially, placing it down next to the ring. "You've done enough for me and I clearly haven't held up my end of the agreement since you don't have a green card. I'm going to assume you're letting that slide since you're dissolving our contract."

His eyes spark and I know he's angry by the tick in his jaw that pulses. Good. I want him to be angry. I want him to feel a fucking shred of the anguish that's twisting my intestines and scraping against my heart.

"Thank you for paying off my loan." I clear my throat. "I

guess we're done here." I offer him a sad smile, taking one last, long look at his devastatingly handsome face.

My chest heaves with a sob of all the things we're going to miss out on.

Then, I turn on my heel and leave the bedroom. I leave Torsten Hansen behind.

My flight to New York is long and tearful. My emotions swing wildly from heartbroken and hurting to angry and defensive.

Why didn't he fight for me?

Did I really read all the signs wrong? Did I fall for an act instead of the man?

No, my heart screams. Obviously, my head scoffs back.

"Would you like a glass of wine?" the sweet flight attendant who has already brought me tissues and chocolate chip cookies from First Class asks when we're somewhere over France.

I give in and nod. I definitely need something to take the edge off. Besides, all my crying and trying not to cry has given me a wicked tension headache that can't be much worse than a hangover.

She squeezes my shoulder empathetically and I hate myself a little for losing it in front of a stranger. On the other hand, it's also a relief because I would abhor being this vulnerable, this pathetic, in front of anyone I care about.

Once I have a wine glass in hand, I take a deep gulp and let my mind wander over the last few days. It's as if I'm searching for clues to understand what the hell went wrong.

When did Torsten decide he knew what was best for me, for us? Why didn't he speak to me about it? How did I read the situation wrong? I thought we were growing together, building the foundation of something special. And he thought, what? That we were becoming great friends who sometimes have amazing sex but will ultimately end up divorced?

I tip my wine glass all the way back, grateful that my row is empty.

As the hours tick by and my erratic emotions calm, new thoughts replace the frantic ones. Like how it was a privilege to meet Farmor. And Magnus sure is one adorable kid. My niece is only a year younger and similarly, I've never met her. Wouldn't it be amazing if I could patch things up with Jesse the way Torsten did with Anders?

Wouldn't it be something if I could mend my relationship with Dad?

Is it even worth it to try at this point? After all these years and so much hurt? Will reaching out help me find closure, help to heal the wounds that still fester? Or will it cut me deeper, make me bleed when I'm starting to scab over?

The flight attendant returns with another glass of wine and I accept it greedily. At 35,000 feet in the air, the wine hits me harder than usual. I'm grateful when my eyelids grow heavy and sleep beckons. Because sleeping means not thinking. Not thinking means not agonizing over Torsten.

Right now, I need to reimagine what my immediate future looks like. I need to think about the life that I want, the career I want to commit myself to, the place I want to live. Making those kind of life-changing decisions requires sleep. Energy. A clear head.

I pass out somewhere over the Atlantic and don't wake up until we're touching down at JFK. While I glance at the New York City skyline as we land, a ripple passes through my chest. It's definitely not excitement but it's not devastation either.

Feeling bold and a little bit reckless after having spiraled so spectacularly, I pull my suitcase off the baggage claim belt and line up for a taxi. When it's my turn, I slip into the back seat of a cab and rattle off my brother's address, a penthouse on Fifth Avenue my dad gifted to him as a wedding present. I haven't been in years but I remember it well.

I remember him and Mira well. Jesse always tried to please Dad. He did everything right, followed the rules, and never rocked the boat. If I'm oil, he's water. But one of my greatest takeaways from Norway is that there's always a road home, even if it's all scorched Earth and an arduous trek. Maybe I need to start remembering instead of trying to forget. Maybe it's time for me to make amends too.

When we pull up to the building, I pay the taxi fare and collect my suitcase. I stand in front of the building, craning my neck all the way back to see the penthouse. The warm spring breeze whips my hair over my shoulders. People rush around me, maybe not even seeing me. I close my eyes and breathe in the city. The sunshine. The anonymity and the freedom and the moment.

I forgot how much I love Manhattan. I forgot how much I adore traveling and experiencing and being. After a year of just trying to survive, I forgot that at one point, I didn't have to try at all.

I smile at the doorman and pull my suitcase behind me.

"Can I help you with something, Ms.?" he asks politely.

I study him for a long moment. "Dale?"

He frowns. "Yes."

I grin. "It's me, Rielle. Jesse's sister."

His eyes widen but he smiles back. "Rielle Carter. Wow. Your brother is going to be delighted to see you."

I laugh in response because that's a stretch but sweet of Dale to say. It's the extra reassurance I need that I'm doing the right thing, that I should step into the elaborately decorated building with its high ceilings and expensive scent. The private elevator, the guest code, the entire ritual brings me back to a million years ago, when Mom and I went to see the New York City Ballet. Her friends had disapproved that it wasn't the American Ballet Theater and I remember how she laughed and laughed, winking at me across the table. Later, we shopped in Chinatown instead of the fancy shops dotted along Fifth. We ate hot dogs from a cart on the street corner and had giant, Mister Softee ice cream cones with sprinkles as a late-night snack. Mom said she wanted me to see the *real* New York and I fell in love with the bold way the city imprinted itself on me. The grit and grind, the colors and scents, the way millions of people milled about with little concern for playing a part. That trip taught me the importance of being, of enjoying, of actively engaging in one's own life and choices. That trip changed the trajectory of my life because after Mom passed, I clung to her laughter and the way her eyes danced, and I channeled it to stand up to Dad.

The elevator doors ping open and my brother is standing there, his arms crossed over his chest and a frown on his face. His eyes are dark like mine, like Dad's. His eyes scan me quickly, lingering too long on my red, puffy eyes.

Then he sighs, "Jesus, Rielle." He reaches out and pulls me straight into an embrace, wrapping his arms around my back and squeezing.

My nose is pressed into the soft material of his shirt and the scent of his cologne, familiar, rushes over me. Tears well in my eyes and for the second time in twenty-four hours, a sob works its way up my throat. I fall apart in my brother's arms but this time, it feels like a homecoming.

"WHAT HAPPENED?" Jesse asks a little while later.

I twirl the spoon in my mug of tea slowly and think about how to answer that. He lifts an impatient eyebrow at me and his wife, Mira, places a hand on his wrist. The nanny whisked little Leah out to the park the moment my presence was known.

"Ri?" he prods and I don't miss the worry that blazes in his eyes.

I sigh, "Which part?"

Jesse pinches the bridge of his nose but Mira turns an understanding gaze my way. "Why don't you tell us what led you here today? Now? We've been hoping you'd connect for years now. After Leah was born..."

A lump grows in my throat and I feel like shit. Sitting across from them now, I can understand the hurt that my disappearance from their lives, from their happy occasions, caused. But in the moment of proving my independence to my father, I never considered how Jesse would feel. I figured he wouldn't care one way or the other. We were never overly close. I was Mom's daughter and he was Dad's son and after Mom passed, I felt like I could never align with the Carter men. But maybe drawing that dividing line was more on me? Did my decision, my choice, fracture us?

I let out a sigh and glance up. Jesse watches me with so much concern, his lips pressed together, his jaw tight, and my chest squeezes. I rack my mind for a moment, a memory, where Jesse and I were truly at odds and I realize there were none. I always assumed he would do Dad's bidding and I desperately wanted to blaze my own trail. Staring at my brother, I realize that I've hurt him just as much as I believed he'd hurt me. I open my mouth, and the whole story tumbles out. College and photography classes and Claire. Jerry Jensen and Stu Sanders and Merck No-Last-Name. Eviction notices and interest rates and unemployment. Torsten Hansen and a magical wedding day, Farmor and a hospital bed, Norway.

When I'm done, Mira has tears streaking down her cheeks. My brother looks like he's going to be physically ill or put his fist through a wall but he does neither of those things. Instead, he opens his arms again and when I hug him, he murmurs, "God I'm glad you're home, Rielle."

I snort-laugh and run my hands over my face. "I never thought I'd come back."

He shakes his head and pulls back. "Dad was always too hard on you. I kept telling him he needed to compromise with you but he truly believed that being a hard ass was the only way to parent." Jesse shrugs. "I know you think I never cared or never got involved. But really, Rielle, I was trying to do everything his way so you wouldn't have to. I know you never wanted the life that came along with Carter Enterprises. You live your life under a microscope with too many fingers in too many pies. I liked it though and thought if I could be great at it, the expectation for you to be involved wouldn't be there. It didn't work out that way."

Surprise rocks through me at his confession. My eyelids drop closed and I recall memories, moments after Mom's death when I was angry and hurting and confused. With Jesse's words ringing in my head, I process them differently. My mind flickers to Torsten and his family business. Was Anders trying to protect him too? Or did the drama, manipulation, and hurt send Torsten running like me? If Jesse and Dad welcomed me back into the family fold right now, would I want to stay? When I open my eyes, I process Torsten's predicament differently. I also see my brother in a whole new light. "I'm sorry, Jesse. I'm so sorry." Remorse is heavy in my tone.

My brother squeezes my shoulder. "I am too, Ri. More than you will ever know." He tips his head to my chair and I sit back down.

Mira reaches across the table and squeezes my hand. I give her a grateful smile.

"Just so you know, Dad kept tabs on you. He was getting ready to intervene right when you threw him a curveball and married the hockey player."

I inhale a sharp breath. "Dad knew?"

My brother snorts. "Carter's Steakhouse?" He mentions the exorbitantly priced steakhouse in downtown Boston.

"That's you guys?"

"It's all of us, Ri. It's a family business. Dad thought you'd eventually come home. He waited freshman year. Then, he thought after college. When he found out that Jerry Jensen was the lender behind your loan, he tried to pay it off outright. He *hated* the thought of you, of any of us, being under Jensen's thumb."

"Jensen refused."

Jesse nods. "Dad was furious. I think his anger is what held him back from reaching out earlier." Jesse leans back in his chair and crosses his arms. "I know you think you're just like Mom, Ri. And you are. You got all of her sunshine and sparkle. You sure as hell got her mischievous side."

I smirk.

"But your pride? Your stubbornness? That rivals Dad's. Neither one of you wanted to take the first step. But when Dad saw, truly saw, how you were living, he called me from the parking lot of your apartment building raging."

"He did?"

Jesse nods.

"Imagine his surprise when he learned you had moved. Had married," Mira offers.

Oh God. I drop my head, imagining the betrayal my father must have felt. The awful guilt that must have settled on his shoulders to learn that his daughter married a stranger instead of reaching out to him.

"Rielle," Mira's voice breaks through my voice. "Why don't you stay for a bit?"

My brow furrows. "Pardon?"

She grins. "Do you have anything to get back to in Boston?"

I shake my head.

"Then stay. Please. Spend some time with Leah, with us. We've missed you."

If the lump in my throat could expand anymore, I'd be suffocating. I swallow past it and nod, tears filling the corners of my eyes. "I'd like that. Thank you."

She squeezes my hand again. "Besides, you shouldn't go through a divorce on your own."

My brother's eyes narrow at the word *divorce.* "You're pretty torn up about a fake marriage."

I look down at the table but see Mira scold him from the corner of my eye.

"What?" he mutters.

I look back up. "I'm in love with him." I declare it to the room even though it makes me look pathetic. My tears make me appear weak. But in many ways, I've already hit rock bottom and anything I say and do now can't possibly make me feel any worse.

Jesse swears but Mira nods, understanding in her eyes. "I know," she says. "So, stay. New York is a great place to lose yourself in when you feel lost."

I nod, thinking over her words.

"Come on, I'll show you to your room." She stands from the table, clasping the handle of my suitcase.

Right before I clear the table, Jesse's hand darts out and wraps around my wrist.

I turn and look at him over my shoulder.

"I'm glad you came here," he says and the conviction in his tone tells me he's serious.

"Me too."

He squeezes my wrist. "But don't ever fucking do that to me again, Ri."

I smile. "I won't, Jes. Promise."

The corner of his mouth tugs up and he drops my hand. I follow Mira to a bedroom they've designated for guests, taking in the pretty white lace bed coverlet and the elegantly framed photos on the walls. Once I'm alone, I lie back on the bed. Exhaustion sweeps through my body and the thud of my heartbeat echoes in my temples.

Jesse's concern and Mira's invitation were definitely not what I was expecting but God, it felt good to belong somewhere. To belong to someone, a family. A flicker of relief catches in my chest that I'm not going to have to navigate this next chapter alone. A shock of warmth blooms in my stomach that all this time, while I was swearing off my dad, he was still watching from afar.

I roll to my side and dig through my purse for my phone.

When I see Torsten's name on the screen, my fingers begin to shake. I swipe right and read the message.

TORSTEN

Please, Ri. Just tell me your safe. Where are you staying?

RIELLE

Make things right with your father.

I text instead, letting him know I'm okay but also upholding my promise to Farmor. Torsten replies immediately.

TORSTEN

Are you okay?

His words cause a fresh wave of pain to crash over me. Will I ever be okay without him? It's only been a handful of hours and my heart misses his so much it aches.

I bite my bottom lip to keep my emotions in check. I've cried more in the past two days than I have in the past two, hell, five years. Now that the dam holding back my feelings has broken, everything I thought I was managing has rushed forward, manifesting through traitorous tears and broken sobs.

RIELLE

No. But I will be.

Then, I dial my dad's number.

"Rielle?" he answers on the first ring.

"Daddy," my voice cracks but the breaks in my heart begin to mend.

CHAPTER TWENTY-TWO
TORSTEN

She's staying in New York.

It's been a week since Rielle walked out of my life and I broke my promise. I let her go. Watching from the window as Lars pulled out of the driveway with her bundled into the back seat haunts me. I miss her warmth, her presence, *her*.

"Hey. You okay?" Anders asks as he comes around the corner. I'm standing by said window, staring at an empty space, wishing the memory of a week ago wasn't playing on a mental loop in my head.

"Yeah." I clear my throat and step away from the window. "I'm fine."

Anders rocks back on his heels. "You shouldn't have run her off like that."

I sigh and scrub my palm over my face. "This life isn't for her."

"Maybe not," he agrees and I look up sharply.

My brother's face is etched with lines of wisdom only gained from personal failures and heartaches.

I lift an eyebrow, waiting for him to continue.

He shrugs. "You didn't give her the choice, the chance, to

come to that conclusion on her own. One thing I know about strong women, they don't like others making decisions for them, dictating their own happiness." He tilts his head toward Father's office. "Come on. He's waiting."

But I don't move. Is that what I did with Rielle? In trying to give her the future she deserves, did I take away her freedom to choose? My hands tighten into fists as I think of my girl, my *wife*, with her tearstained face and pleading eyes.

"Torsten?" Anders calls.

I nod and follow him to meet Father.

Rielle's text blares in my mind. I need to make amends. I swore to Farmor that I would. I promised Rielle I'd follow through. I need to set things right with Father and then I could lose myself in thoughts of Rielle, can admit how much I fucking miss her.

"Father." I slip into the office and close the door behind me.

He's seated behind his desk, his eyes so pale they're nearly translucent. But they're ringed in hardness and bitterness and for a blink, I catch a glimpse of what I'll look like in thirty-some years if I let the anger eat my soul.

He stares at me long and hard, as if seeing me for the first time. I sink into the chair opposite his desk, remembering all the times I was scolded in this exact chair for silly little things that children do. Running in the hallways, stealing biscuits from the kitchen, putting a frog in Anders' bed…

"She always loved you best." His voice shakes me from my thoughts and I meet his gaze. In them, I see a sliver of regret but it's overshadowed by his genuine dislike for me. "The best Hansen," he scoffs.

I straighten in my seat, realization and shock racing through my veins. "You were…*jealous*?"

"She left you the company!" he hollers, banging his fist on the top of his desk.

Next to me, Anders flinches. But I've spent too many years on the ice, surrounded by tough guys fueled by testosterone and competitive edges to be rattled by his posturing.

I nod, working a swallow. "She did. She left me the company even *after* you tried to smear my reputation, my name. You tried to cut me off from our entire family and still, Farmor saw you for what you are."

"Torsten," Anders warns next to me.

I came in here to make amends. But how the hell can we even begin to heal if we don't address our hurts?

I wait for Father's outburst but he surprises me again by slumping back in his chair, his eyes closing as if in pain. Is he upset because he's losing the company? Or is he truly saddened that he was such a colossal disappointment to the greatest woman on Earth?

"You're right," he says finally.

Anders inhales sharply beside me.

"You love Magnus," I say suddenly.

Father's eyes narrow. "What?"

"I've seen you with him. You're...kinder. More giving than you ever were with us." I gesture between Anders and me.

Father rubs the space between his eyes. "He's my grandson."

"I know. We're your sons."

His eyes harden. "I know." His tone is clipped.

"I don't want to keep living like this. With no family, no ties. And I won't do to you what you did to me. I won't do it to a little boy who clearly admires you either." I watch Father carefully, committing this moment to memory. I don't want to live my life with burdens on my soul, with regrets in my blood. I want to move forward with a clear conscience and a family to call mine. "You step away from the business. Let the next generation of Hansen men have our crack at it. If we need your help, we'll ask. But you don't get involved. Take your settlement, spend some time abroad, let this wound heal and not fester. And when you're ready to be a grandfather and a father and a real friend, come home. There will be a place here waiting for you."

His mouth drops open even though his eyes flash. He doesn't want to believe me, he doesn't know how to trust that I'm extending an olive branch, and it's stamped all over his face. "What's the catch?" he asks after a moment.

I chuckle humorlessly. "There is no catch."

"There's always a catch."

"No." I shake my head. "There's always a choice. And I'm choosing to forgive you. Want the truth?" I lift my chin at him. "I don't want to be you in thirty years, sitting behind a desk in a cold office, having dragged every piece of good in my life through so much shit that the stench won't wash away."

Anders' head whips to mine and I feel his eyes boring into the side of my face. But I keep my eyes on Father.

"I forgive you, Father. For everything. And I'd like to be able to look up to you one day. But that day isn't today. It won't be tomorrow either. You need to go and figure out what you want." I stand from my chair. "For what it's worth, I hope you come back when you're ready."

He watches me for a long moment and sighs heavily.

"Farmor was right," Anders says softly.

"About?" I ask.

"You are the best Hansen."

Father scoffs. Anders' observation hangs in the air for a moment before Father clears his throat and begrudgingly nods in agreement.

I snort and hold out a hand. Father stands on the other side of the desk and hesitates for a moment before placing his hand in mine and shaking.

"I'll be seeing you, Torsten."

"I hope so," I tell him. Then, I turn on my heel and leave Father's office.

I stride back to my bedroom, my hands nearly shaking. I've never stood up to Father before but God, does it feel good, to get some of the feelings I kept locked away for decades out in the open. I'm not daft. I know rebuilding a relationship with Father will take time. I also know it will never truly be the relationship I'd like it to be because we have too much hurt in our history. But I feel a ribbon of hope for what my family could look like in the future. Father, Anders, Magnus, Uncle Erik, Johan, Daniel, and me. A bunch of searching men forever held together by our love for the woman who made us. Farmor.

I sit on the edge of my mattress, my chest tight. I miss her. I miss her sparkling eyes and her light laughter. I miss her warm embrace and her wise advice. The image of Rielle holding her hand that night in the hospital slips into my mind, unbidden.

If Farmor were here, I know she'd be urging me to make things right with Rielle. But how can I when I hurt her so badly?

I pull out my phone and text her before I can second-guess it.

TORSTEN

It's done. I spoke to Father.

RIELLE

Proud of you.

My throat thickens at her message. Of course she is. Even now, hurting, she has my back and proves her loyalty. It aches and soothes at the same time and more than anything, I wish she was here so I could wrap my arms around her, take her to my bed, and show her all the things I don't know how to say with words.

TORSTEN

Are you okay?

RIELLE

No. But I will be.

I frown at her words, the same from last week. I hired a guy to keep an eye on her in New York. I'm sure she'd hate it if she knew but there's no way I can be here, in Oslo, and not know she's safe in New York. I know she's been spending hours around the city, getting lost in Central Park, taking photographs. I know she's had lunch with her father twice and is staying with her brother and his family, which made me smile. Not for the first time, I realize just how much I don't know about my wife, her past, and the choices she wants to make for her future.

And I hate myself a little bit for not learning them all sooner.

ANOTHER WEEK without Rielle passes and it nearly destroys me. My hands reach for her in my sleep, my thoughts circle around her during the day, and my heart craves hers.

But tying her down to me, a man who's relocating to Norway, a guy who needs to rebuild so many bridges with his family, a person who is financially secure, emotionally stunted, and mentally drained, isn't fair. Not when she's on the cusp of her life. Her twenties have barely gotten started. She hasn't had the time to explore the kind of future she wants, to find the type of man who deserves to be by her side.

If I've learned one thing in my time married to Rielle Carter, it's that I'm not deserving enough. Not if I would drag her to Oslo, ask her to confront my farmor, and then push her away. Not if I would choose to stay behind and deal with my family business bullshit while she boarded a plane headed for the States.

The only silver lining to my heartache is that things in Oslo, at Hansen Manor, are so twisted that I lose myself in the business, my family, and preserving Magnus's legacy. The week after we bury Farmor, I spend a solid twenty-four hours drunk out of my mind. Anders, Daniel, Johan, and I sit on the back deck of the Manor and pass a bottle, then two, of whiskey, the good stuff, around. We get rip-roaringly drunk. The kind of drunk that serves as a truth serum. Shit from our childhoods, grudges we've held on to, hurts we've kept buried, all bubble to the surface and float away with the sunset at nearly 10 p.m.

The four of us spring into action in the following week since Uncle Erik and Father have stepped aside. Father is spending some time in France while Uncle Erik went to visit a friend in the Middle East. It feels like we all breathe a little easier with them out of Norway. Even though Father and I spoke, it feels necessary to put some emotional distance between us.

His absence leaves me with more time to focus on my other relationships. Like gaining back my brother and my cousins. Like spending time with my amazing nephew, a little mini me, who loves hockey and skating, and looks at me with stars in his eyes.

I focus on all of this and try to ignore the dull throb in my chest where my heart used to be. Any thought of Rielle sets me back, distracts me, causes me to turn a million what-ifs and if-onlys over in my mind. During the day, I try to block her out, but it's impossible. Everything I see somehow reminds me of a memory associated with her. Eating smoked salmon, a childhood staple, now has me recalling that first breakfast I made her in our kitchen. By the end of each day, I'm desperate for sleep to claim me just to ease the longing in my chest. Still, she finds me in my dreams.

Twelve days after she left, I can't take it anymore. I cave and dial her number.

Listening to the phone ring has my nerves bouncing around, eager and insecure and hopeful.

"Torsten?" Her voice comes through the line and I clench the phone. I take a moment to let her voice wash over me and it's even better than I remembered.

"Hey Ri," I murmur.

"You okay?" The concern is heavy in her tone and it causes emotion to swell inside of me because if she answered my call, does that mean she still cares?

"I miss you," I admit. "I miss you every second of every day."

She sucks in an audible inhale and I pause, giving her time to collect her thoughts.

"I miss you too, Torst." Her words are exactly what I want to hear but the emotion underlining them, the hurt and the thinly veiled anger, causes my stomach to twist.

"I shouldn't have pushed you away, Ri. You were right when you said I didn't ask what you wanted. I thought I knew better and I did what I thought was best without ever considering your thoughts." I blurt out the truth, needing her to know that I realize just how epically I messed things up between us.

"Yeah," she whispers. "It seems to be a theme in my life." I frown but before I can ask, she volunteers the information. "My dad."

"Are you guys talking again?" I ask, even though I already know the answer. I should tell her I've had eyes on her since she landed in New York but right now, I don't want to rock the boat. The truth is, I'll never not worry about Rielle. Panic seized me when she left Norway with no access to cash, no plan, no nothing. Immediately, I called a guy I know in the city to keep an eye on her. He keeps assuring me she's fine and still, I can't let her safety go.

"Yes. We've been spending some time together. I'm staying with Jesse, my brother, in the city. Reconnecting with my family has been good for me."

"Good. That's great, Rielle. I'm…I'm really happy for you."

"I'm happy for you, too. Mending things with your dad, fulfilling your promise to Farmor." Her voice cracks and I wince.

"Yeah," I agree after a moment.

She's quiet for a long beat. "Too bad we couldn't fight hard enough to fix us, huh?"

The sadness in her voice squeezes me like a vice. "Rielle, I—"

"Made your choice," she finishes for me.

"Don't think. Just answer. What's your choice?" I blurt out, my curiosity getting the better of me. My fingers nearly tremble from clenching the phone so tightly.

She sighs. "Me. Right now, I choose myself. I have to."

Disappointment rocks through me even though on some level, her answer pleases me. I want her to put herself first. It's what I've always wanted for her. But then why the hell does her confirming it hurt?

"Good, sweetheart. You deserve everything. The best."

"That's what I keep hearing."

I flinch at the hint of sarcasm in her tone. "Rielle—"

"I'm not okay, Torsten. But I'm getting there." She disconnects the call.

I hold the phone in my hand and stare at it.

An incoming email from Bill lights up my screen.

Subject: Divorce papers?

I swear and throw my phone down on the bed.

I'm in love with my wife. I love Rielle Carter Hansen. And even though I have to, I don't want to divorce her. I want her forgiveness and her love. I want to be her choice.

At the beginning of June, I fly back to Boston to sit on the bench and cheer on the Hawks as we play in the Stanley Cup Finals.

"Missed you, man!" Panda smacks me on the back when I enter the locker room. A general cheer goes up and I grin and thank the guys for welcoming me back with open arms.

I know if it wasn't me, a guy who's given most of my life to this team, and I wasn't injured, I wouldn't have been given the green light from the Hawks to stay in Norway and settle Farmor's estate. But now, the team knows I'm not returning, that this is my last season, and that my life is headed in a new direction, across the Atlantic.

To be received so warmly from the men who've been my family for more years than my own is touching and fills me with emotion. I sigh; I am getting too damn soft in my old age.

James wraps an arm around my neck and for the first time, I think I understand a fraction of the sheer devastation he felt losing Layla. Because of Claire, I know Rielle is happy and whole, working at a photography studio in New York. Her happiness brings me comfort. To think the world could spin without Rielle would gut me and I realize now just how broken my old friend is.

I place James in a headlock and he laughs, punching me softly in the ribs. "Don't want to hurt you, old man."

I snort and drop my hold.

James lifts his chin at me. "How are you holding up? All healed?"

I nod, letting my shoulder rotate. It still clicks and cracks but it's functioning again. Not that I'll ever skate onto the ice as an NHL Hawk and give it a test, but it works for my everyday use. "Knee's doing okay too," I tell him.

"Good. It's good to see you."

"I'll be cheering louder than anyone in the stands for you guys tonight." I smack the back of Easton's head.

He turns to me and grins. "Don't waste up all your lung capacity in one go. It's only the first game of the series."

I flip him the middle finger but agree, "Fair enough."

Easton watches me curiously for a long beat and drops his voice. "She's doing okay, man."

My chest seizes at the mention of Rielle, even though he didn't say her name. My guy still gives me regular updates about Rielle's safety but it's not the same as knowing her thoughts. I think of her all the time and wonder how she's coping with her new norm, her relationships with her family members. "You sure?"

"Yeah. She's happy in New York. Claire misses her fiercely, but Ri needed this separation from Boston. From reminders of you."

I frown at his word choice. Does she hate me that much? Will she ever forgive me for the sham of a marriage I dragged her through?

"Rielle needed a change of scenery. Some time to grow. Some time to heal," East continues, tapping me on the chest as he stows the last of his belongings in his locker. "Let's go win the Cup."

I tip my head and force a grin. "Hell yeah."

I follow the team out to the ice and breathe in the cold air, holding it in my lungs. I take in the cheering crowd, the excited expressions, the jerseys the fans rock. Some of them still represent with my number and it's humbling. Sure, this isn't how I saw it all going down but Bill was right. I had one hell of a career.

I sit on the bench in my jersey and cheer on my team for the entire game. I give East a few pointers, I remind James of some of his opponent's strengths, I commend Noah on a beautiful breakaway. In a way, coming back for the Finals is the closure I needed. Because I can tell from my seat on the bench, that part of me has already moved on. Now that hockey is over, now that Rielle is gone, there's nothing holding me here except memories. And even though the majority of them are great, the ones that aren't hurt so deeply, they shadow the good times.

We beat Dallas and a victory cry rocks the arena.

Maybe I'm not on the ice but by the hugs and back slaps from my teammates, I recognize that my presence still matters to them. I'm still helping the team reach for a Cup win.

OVER THE NEXT week and a half, I spend all my free time at the arena. I help the guys prepare for every game against the Diamonds that I can. I'm able to skate a bit and help them set up the plays Coach Phillips wants to work out.

Late at night, while Boston sleeps, I check in with Anders as he drinks his morning coffee. We run through the financials, discuss investment opportunities, and brainstorm ways to make our archaic family company more socially responsible and environmentally conscious. It's definitely not the work I anticipated for myself after hanging up my skates but a part of me enjoys it. I like working with my brother and cousins more than I thought I would. I like connecting with my family again.

With my time in Boston coming to a close, I consider selling the penthouse. I consider selling my Waterfront properties. I meet with a brokerage and discuss different scenarios but in the end, I can't do it. I can't cut ties with the city. I can't move on from a place I've considered home for too long.

And despite my reaching out to Bill, I definitely can't bring myself to ask him to draft up divorce papers.

Instead, I pour my days into hockey, into the Hawks. My nights into my family and the prosperity of the Hansens. I throw myself into everything and anything to blunt the hurt of losing Rielle. Still, she finds me in my dreams and I wake up longing for her the same way I used to before I ever had her. Now, it just hurts more.

On game six of the series, the team's nerves are on high alert. We're leading the series 3–2 and this game will determine if we win the Cup outright or need to play game seven for a tiebreaker. For some strange reason I don't understand, I'm even more nervous sitting on the side than I would be skating onto the ice.

I take my spot on the bench, exchange a few words with Coach Phillips, and turn my eyes to the ice when I feel it. The sensation of someone watching me. The back of my neck chills and a strange sense of awareness spreads through my body. I turn my head and glance over my shoulder, my eyes scanning the crowd. On a whim, as if I can't help myself, my attention travels to the WAGs box.

Midnight eyes clasp onto mine and I freeze, my limbs locking down. Her hair is longer, wilder. Her lips are painted red and her eyes are so dark, their depths are unfathomable. She's rocking my number and staring at me with an intensity that's more like a gravitational force. I can't look away. And I don't want to.

The arena, the game, the nerves, every single thing it took to get me to this point in my life, to this moment, fade away. There's her and there's me and there's us. Our story which once had the potential to be my favorite but is still one I'd choose all over again.

A slow smile spreads across her mouth and she lifts her hand in the tiniest of waves. Hesitant, vulnerable, and so fucking real, she makes the first move.

I pounce on it and wave back. I gesture to her that we'll share a drink after the game. Fans stretching the distance between us turn and stare, following our exchange with interest. Rielle laughs and it's like staring directly at the sun. Bright, blinding, so beautiful it burns. She nods and mimes lining up a row of shot glasses.

Fans' necks swivel back to me as I chuckle and pretend to toss back the shots. Our eye contact never breaks and over the heads of hundreds of people, we have a conversation that only we understand.

I give her a wink and turn back to the ice in time to watch the puck drop. Game six is one of the most intense, brutal, and awe-inspiring games I've ever witnessed. Austin scores a natural hat-trick, three goals in succession, that has both fans and haters on their feet with their mouths open. Claire, Indy, and Rielle dance in their seats, waving their hands wildly.

In the second period, Panda dives for the puck and knocks it off the side post for a save that fills my chest with relief. Easton weaves through opponents like a demon, Noah has four successful assists, and James play like he did before Layla died—with his full attention, all of his talent, and every bit of his heart.

When the final buzzer rings out and the Hawks win the Stanley Cup, emotion rocks me hard. We did it. We won. But more than that, I realize that my team is going to be okay without me. Just as they should be. I watch as the guys sitting with me on the bench rush the ice. I push off after them, gliding over the ice and throwing myself into the team celebrations.

When Austin is awarded the Stanley Cup, he doesn't hoist it overhead like tradition dictates. Instead, he points to me, skates over, and passes me the trophy. I shake my head at him but he grins. "Congratulations, Torst. Thanks for getting us here."

My hands tremble as I lift the trophy overhead. The team's cheers are deafening. The jubilee of the crowd shakes the arena. My eyes find my wife and hold her gaze.

In a handful of moments, I realize just how much my life has changed. And just how okay I am with it all.

I know the moment he enters Taps because a cheer works through the crowd. Fans whisper excitedly, some ask him for autographs or selfies, and everyone tracks his movement as he makes his way to the bar. To me.

Claire and Indy are already in the private room at the back. Claire's mom, Mary, has decorated the space with balloons and streamers and every throwback decoration you can imagine to make these big, brawny hockey guys feel the same magic of their childhood hockey wins. It's sweet and thoughtful and something I know the team will revel in.

But I stayed out front so I could remember this moment. The one where my husband walked through the door as a hometown hero. The one where I still got to enjoy calling him my husband, if only for a tiny bit longer. I waffled back and forth on whether to come to the game or not. But at Claire's pleading and Mira's urging, I booked a flight. I need to see if there's anything between Torsten and me worth salvaging. Because my choice is him. Once he confirms that I'm not his, that he doesn't see a way for us to move forward together, I can sign divorce papers with a clear head.

But if there's any chance that he'd choose me back… Well, I'm not willing to keep living my life on my own assumptions. I witnessed firsthand how that ruined my relationships with my brother and dad and I don't want to ruin everything with Torsten if there's still hope.

He stops next to me and his eyes flash. I grin at him and bring my wine glass to my lips.

"What're you drinking, Ri?"

"Just a merlot."

His smile widens. "Just a merlot, huh?"

"Congrats on the win."

"Thank you."

"You earned it," I tell him the truth, my voice laced with emotion.

He must hear the nervous thread in my tone because his smile slips a little. "You came to the game."

"I wanted to see you accept the trophy."

"How'd you know we'd win tonight?"

I take a sip of my wine. "If you didn't, I would have been at game seven."

"That right?" he asks, his arm wrapping around my waist. "You want to relocate to the back?"

I nod, knowing this is a big night for him. More than anything, Torsten and I need to talk. He still hasn't sent me divorce papers. I never went back to the penthouse. He has my belongings and I have his last name and everything between us is a big, complicated mess. But tonight isn't the night to hammer out those details. Tonight, I want him to celebrate with his teammates and smile at me like he's truly happy I'm here. Like he is right now.

He leads me to the back room and everyone stands and claps. Even though Torsten didn't play in the Finals, everyone knows this is his last season. Tonight was his last game as a Hawk. If anyone has helped the team progress over the past two decades, it's been Torsten, and I love seeing him receive the recognition he's earned. I love the blush that works over his cheeks and the gratitude in his voice when he thanks the group even more.

I sidle up to the bar as Torsten is pulled into congratulatory hugs and photographs with his teammates and their families. East takes the barstool next to mine and orders a club soda.

"Big night for you." I bump my hip against his. "Congratulations."

"Thanks, Ri. Glad you decided to come out for the game."

"Me too."

"You talk to him yet?" He tips his head toward Torsten.

"It's not the night for that."

"Oh, please." Claire appears at my other side, sandwiching me between her and Easton. "As if he's going to let you walk out of Taps tonight without knowing exactly where you guys stand."

"I need to know where we stand too." My voice wavers and I clear my throat. "Either we're married for real or we're done for good."

East snorts and takes a gulp of his club soda.

Claire straight up laughs.

I glare at her.

She shrugs. "Ri-Ri, I fucking adore you. But sometimes you can be so thick."

"What?" I swat at her arm but she catches my hand and holds on to it.

"Torsten is a man of means. I mean, come on, look at him."

We both turn toward him and I drink him in greedily, memorizing the breadth of his shoulders, the slant of his cheekbones, the shape of his mouth.

"If he wanted to divorce you, you would have been divorced weeks ago," Claire mutters beside me. "The truth is staring you straight in the face. That man is head over heels in love with you. He just thinks you don't love him back."

I whip my head toward her and frown. "That's ridiculous. I—"

"Have you told him, point blank, how you feel?" East asks from my other side.

"What?" I face him, my head spinning.

"We don't always get it," East cuts me off. "Sometimes, it takes us guys longer to catch up to what's really happening. But Torsten isn't like most guys. He's more caring, more empathetic. If you didn't spell it out for him, then he'll keep believing that he trapped you into something you agreed to for a fresh start."

My mouth opens and closes several times.

East shoots me an apologetic grin. "Take another sip of your wine, Ri."

"Yeah, you're gonna need it," Claire advises.

I look up and see the confusion streak across Torsten's face as his eyes scan mine. Then, he's striding toward me. His expression is fierce, his body strong. A Norse Viking with the soul of an Ancient Greek philosopher. Until I met him, I didn't think men like him existed. How could they?

He stops in front of me and East and Claire make themselves scarce.

"What's wrong?" he asks me.

I gaze up into his pale blue eyes. "What's right?"

A flicker of recognition ripples over his expression. "Ri—"

"I'm in love with you, Torsten Hansen," I blurt out. "I know this isn't the time to say it. I know tonight is your night. But before you hand me divorce papers and before I fly back to New York, I want you to know the truth that I am terrified to admit to you. I am in love with you. I have been for weeks. This past month was the best and worst of my life. I missed you so fucking much it hurt to breathe. But I learned a lot."

He licks his bottom lip. His eyes bore into mine and his hands wrap around my upper arms. "What did you learn?"

I take a deep inhale. "I learned that your eyes are the same pale, sky blue as the sunrise in Manhattan in springtime. I learned that my default is to push people away, and it's never too late to go home. You taught me that and after Oslo, I went to my brother's house and met my niece. I learned that as much as I love caramel macchiato coffee drinks, I actually prefer tea parties in tutus. I learned that I'm a city girl through and through. I can get drunk off a pretty skyline and some gritty hustle. Photography is more than an interest, it's my passion. And I learned that I don't want to live my life without you in it. I want to be your wife, for real. Because what I feel for you…" I shrug, tears brushing the tops of my cheeks. "It's not going away and I can't make it. I know because I've tried."

His hands squeeze my arms and his eyes blaze and swim and burn with thoughts and feelings and *things*. He shuffles closer until I'm inhaling his exhales, my heart racing in anticipation of whatever he's going to say.

He doesn't say anything. Instead, he pulls me close and kisses me. It's one of those all-consuming, reckless, intense, passionate kisses I used to dream of when I still believed in fairy tales. Torsten's kiss eradicates my insecurities and fills me up with hope. He breaks our connection and smiles down at me. The room is too quiet but neither of us turns to look at the reactions at the free entertainment we're providing.

It seems that Taps is our place and I need to rethink my stance on fairy tales because Torsten gets down on his knee for the third time in my presence and says, "Rielle Carter Hansen, I couldn't let you go if I tried. I know, because I tried. Don't hate me, sweetheart, but I've had eyes on you since you landed in New York. I spent every day we were apart thinking of you, missing you. I love you and I want you any way I can have you. I don't care if we live in Boston or New York or Oslo. I don't care if you wear pencil skirts and head to a downtown office or hang in ripped jeans with a camera around your neck. I just want you to be happy. I want all your dreams to come true. But you're my dream. You are my home and we both know, there's nothing like a homecoming." He tugs something from his pocket and a gasp falls from my mouth when I recognize Farmor's ring. He grins sheepishly. "I've been carrying it around in my pocket, as a reminder, hoping I'd find my way back to my love. To you." He slips it on my finger and stands beside me. "Don't take it off again, sweetheart. It's yours and you're mine."

I laugh as Torsten's fingers dry the tears on my cheeks and he brushes his lips over mine.

"A toast," James calls out, raising a beer in the air. Everyone in the room follows suit. They watch us with interest and excitement, with goofy grins and knowing eyes. "To Torsten Hansen, a Hawks legend, a phenomenal team-mate, a solid friend, a man we affectionately call Big Daddy." A few titters sound out but James's eyes are serious when they settle on mine. "To Rielle Hansen, the woman who made our guy whole. May your future be filled with love and happiness."

The team and their loved ones drink to our happily-ever-after and I dip my head, in gratitude and a little embarrassed by all the attention. But Torsten wraps his arm around my waist, his hand splayed over my hip. "Enjoy it, baby. I never gave you a proper wedding."

I glance up at him, incredulous. "You gave me a magical wedding."

"That so?" He winks. "Then you're not going to believe what's in store for the honeymoon."

I tip my head back and laugh. Torsten smiles. Our eyes latch and the world falls away, the way it always does when it's us.

"Ours is my favorite story," he murmurs, reading my thoughts.

Then, he kisses me and I fall even deeper in love with my husband.

EPILOGUE

TORSTEN

TWO MONTHS LATER

August in New York City is sweltering. But since it means Rielle walks around our apartment in tiny shorts that show off her legs and barely-there slips of shirts that leave nothing to the imagination, I'm not in a hurry to get back to Oslo.

"What do you think of these?" she asks, clicking away at her laptop. Over the summer, Rielle has opened her own photography business. She reached out to her old college professor. Between his connections and Rielle's brother's and father's networks, she's drummed up a considerable amount of business in a short amount of time.

"I like this one." I point to a black and white photo of the groom when he gets his first look at his bride. She was walking down the aisle toward him but in the picture, we only see his reaction. His emotion is raw and real and beautiful. And my girl captured it all, making the happy couple's precious moment timeless.

"It's one of my favorites too," she agrees, scrolling through more photos.

Settling back into life with Rielle is as natural as breathing.

Since we both know what we want, are already married, and have no intention of being apart again, the logistics of our lives weren't too hard to figure out either. For now, as Rielle builds her photography business, a profession that allows location mobility, we've decided to split our time between New York and Oslo.

I've realigned my family's business so that Anders, Johan, Daniel, and myself all control a quarter of the company. We've drawn up some pretty clear policies on how to handle future disputes and disagreements but I'm all for Magnus making any final decisions. Especially since he turns five next month and already shows more promise than the rest of us Hansens combined. Rielle says it shows my emotional maturity that I'm ready to pass the title of the best Hansen on. And Magnus, he's really something else.

"Sweetheart." I set an iced caramel macchiato I whipped up with my fancy espresso machine that I recently learned how to navigate by Rielle's elbow. "We need to leave in an hour if we're going to be on time for dinner at your dad's."

"Yep." She nods. "I'm just going to finish editing this photo."

"Okay." I leave her to her work and wander through our small, Lower East Side apartment. It's in a trendy area, surrounded by fashion boutiques and wine bars. Even though we're here, we've kept our investments in Boston as just that, investments.

Slowly, Rielle and I are learning how to navigate our complicated families and our twisted histories with them. Rielle's brother, Jesse, and his wife, Mira, have welcomed us into their lives wholeheartedly. Rielle adores spending time with her niece, Leah. Now, we're working on repairing her relationship with her father which is slowly improving, facilitated by weekly family dinners and Leah's irresistible charm. Her grandpa is wrapped around her little finger and her three-year-old presence has smoothed out a lot of could-be-awkward moments.

I enter our bedroom, taking a moment to appreciate the framed photo Rielle hung up of our wedding day. We're kissing and it's brimming with passion. Anyone who glances at the photo would have no idea we weren't in love. Because the truth is, pieces of us already were. We just didn't know it yet. I dress for dinner. Once I'm ready, I call out a thirty-minute warning to Rielle.

I love how happy she is. I love seeing her immersed in her photography, something that brings her immense joy. The photos she took of Oslo's stunning nature and Magnus's goofy face on their outing together are some of my favorites. But each week, she improves her skills, and I'm certain that she's going to be a highly sought-after photographer in both New York and Norway in no time.

Maybe even in Greece.

I double-check that our passports are in my carry-on backpack.

While Rielle is preoccupied with her work, I roll out our one shared suitcase and tell her I'll be right back. She hums in approval, never bothering to turn around, as I run our suitcase down to the trunk of our SUV.

She doesn't know this but tonight, after our family dinner, we're heading straight to the airport.

I promised my wife a honeymoon and I am a man of my word. We're going to Santorini, Greece for two weeks of sunrises and sunsets, seafood and swimming, and a chance to learn more about each other.

Even though, right from day one, I've known all the parts of Rielle I needed to.

All of this is just bonus.

When I enter the apartment, she's changing into a sundress. Her hair is wild and loose, just the way I like it. She turns around, scanning the floor.

"What's wrong?" I ask.

"I can't find my shoes. You know, those strappy sandals with the crystals in them?"

"Hm…" I shrug. I packed them.

"I guess I'll just wear these." She slides into some simple flats.

"Looks good to me." I grin.

She steps toward me and I wrap my arms around her waist, my fingers lacing together at the base of her spine. She tilts her head, her eyes studying me.

"You okay, sweetheart?"

"I am. Sometimes it still seems too good to be true."

"What does?"

"Our happily-ever-after."

I nod, knowing exactly what she means. "But it's ours, Ri. It's our story."

"And our story is the best one."

"Damn straight." I kiss her, wondering if I'll ever get enough of this woman.

Probably not but the good news is, I don't have to.

Because my happily-for-now truly grew into a happily-ever-after.

THANK you so much for reading Torsten and Rielle's marriage of convenience. I fell in love with their romance and I hope you did too!

ARE you wondering what's in store for Austin Merrick? The Hawks Captain is in for a surprise when his childhood friend, Chloe Crawford, returns to Boston looking nothing like the girl-next-door from his teenage years. *The Rule Maker* is out now!

IN HIGH SCHOOL, **Austin Merrick was a rule-breaking, hockey star.** Now, he's captain of the NHL Boston Hawks and my last-minute wedding date as I face my ex-fiancé.

WITH A DEVILISH SMIRK and wicked blue eyes, Austin is just as charismatic as I remember. **But this version doesn't break rules. He makes them. Even when I wish he wouldn't...**

TURN the page for a sneak peek.

THE RULE MAKER

CHAPTER ONE - CHLOE

"I've officially regressed," I lament to my best friend Abbi, as I kick my feet up on my bedroom wall. My bedroom wall in my parents new house in Boston because at the ripe age of thirty, I've moved back in.

"It's just temporary, Chlo. Just until you get back on your feet," she reassures me.

I sigh, staring up the ceiling fan which turns lazily, breaking the streams of light that flicker across the room. "I'm back in my childhood hometown, in a house eerily similar to my childhood home, being treated like a child, all because I —"

"Stop," Abbi cuts me off. "Don't go there. You didn't do anything wrong. *Steve* deserves the blame, not you."

Just hearing my ex-fiancé's name feels like a hot, fire iron is being plunged into my chest. Two months ago, Steve blew up our lives and the tidy, perfect future I'd envisioned for us. I never thought he'd cheat on me and most certainly not with Brittney, one of my most trusted and beloved friends, who rounded out the trio along with Abbi and me.

"And Brittney," Abbi adds, as if reading my thoughts. The disgust in her voice alleviates some of the ache in my chest.

At least I still have Abbi, who was quick to cut Steve and

Brittney off despite my delusional desire to make things okay between us all. *It's just the hurt talking*, Abbi said. She was right. As the weeks passed and Brittney moved into the airy, inviting, farmhouse-styled apartment I decorated in Hoboken, New Jersey, my hurt seeped into anger. Anger tinged with humiliation.

How dare my fiancé and friend have an affair behind my back? Were they planning to keep it up after Steve and I wed? Would I have ever caught on if Abbi didn't surprise me with a day of pampering for my birthday and I forgot my flip-flops for my pedicure at home?

The thought of Steve and Brittney going at it like rabbits on *my* bed, with the wood paneled headboard and white coverlet from Pottery Barn, flares in my mind like a trumpet. I groan.

Abbi sighs. "Babe, I know you're hurt."

"I'm not hurt. I'm furious," I correct her, wishing I could bleach my eyeballs to unsee everything I saw. "I'm so angry and pissed off and —" tears well in my eyes — "*hurt.*" I agree with Abbi's assessment. "I don't know what to do with all these dumb feelings." I swipe the tears away with the backs of my knuckles. "I hate that *they're* living their best lives in my home while I've been banished to Boston."

Abbi clucks at my dramatics and I know she's gearing up to give me some tough love. I bang my heels against the bedroom wall. I'm in desperate need of tough love but that doesn't mean I want to hear it.

"Chloe," Abbi says patiently and in this moment, I love my best friend for helping me navigate these murky waters for the past few months, "you're not banished anywhere. You're taking a break from your life to sort out your next moves. You love Boston. Now, you get to spend the summer with your family in your old stomping grounds. You can visit your mimi and take her out to brunch. And when I come to visit, we'll go clubbing and do a bunch of touristy shit."

"You'll really come?" My voice is small and that's another thing I hate. Since I learned the truth about Steve and Brittney, everything I thought I knew shifted. My perspective changed and in a matter of minutes, I lost some of my confidence. Instead, I feel shaky, like the ground beneath my feet is constantly moving. In short, I've become a less-than-independent, needier version of myself who I simultaneously despise and cling to. I'm blaming that on Steve too.

"Of course I'll come. I hate that I'm missing the engagement party but I'll see you at Marissa's bachelorette next month and I'll extend my Boston visit then."

"Shit." My breath lodges in my throat at the reminder. How did I forget that Marissa Swanson, one of mine and Brittney's and Abbi's friends, is marrying Adam Wright, one of Steve's closest friends, at the end of the summer? "Shit, shit, shit." I bang my heels again.

"You forgot about Marissa's bachelorette? Don't worry, I'll —"

"I forgot about the engagement party!" It's next weekend in Martha's Vineyard. After my relationship imploded, Marissa begged me to stay on as a bridesmaid, despite the awkward tension between Brittney and me. Not wanting to sacrifice another friend, I agreed and now I am majorly regretting that decision. "I need a date."

"You need a hot, hulking, sexy —"

"Where do I find one of those?" I cut Abbi off, panic edging my tone. How did I forget about Marissa's engagement party? My entire summer pretty much revolves around her wedding festivities.

When the daughter of a hotel tycoon and the son of a New York City hedgefund CEO decide they don't want to wait for their marital bliss, people spring into action. In a mere week, venues magically become available and designers personally called Marissa about her wedding dress. At first, when I was still engaged to Steve, I found my friend's ability to cram an engagement party, a bachelorette bash, and a high profile wedding into ten weeks, exciting and romantic.

Now that I'm painfully single, I'm furious with Marissa for forcing me to find a date to two separate events — her engagement party next week and her wedding at the end of the summer. How am I going to face *Steve and Brittney* not once, but twice?

"We can rent one," Abbi tosses out.

I roll my eyes. "I doubt that. Besides, I'd need to rent the same one twice if I want people to think I have a real relationship and not a pity date."

"Do you want people to think you're in a real relationship?"

"More than I want them to think it's a pity date," I say, exasperated.

"Fair enough." Abbi is silent for a long moment. "Drew?"

"I'm not taking my *brother* to a wedding."

"He's hot."

"You're making this worse, not better," I say impatiently.

"Too bad he lives in Texas," Abbi continues as if I haven't spoken at all. If she keeps up, I'll need bleach for my eyes *and* ears.

A knock at my bedroom door draws my attention as Dad pops his head in. His smile is gentle, his eyes warm and I have the sudden urge to hug my dad tightly and cry into his strong chest the same way I did as a little girl. The same way I did two months ago after chucking my engagement ring at Steve's head.

"We're heading to the Merrick's in an hour," Dad reminds me.

I nod, pointing to the phone.

He nods and dips out of my room.

"Abbi, I gotta go. We're heading to a family friend's house for dinner tonight."

"Oh, see! You have a social life," she says way too excitedly.

I snort. Dinner at the Merricks is hardly a social event but considering I've barely interacted with the human species in the past two months, I'm not an accurate judge. "I'll call you tomorrow."

"Have fun tonight."

"'Bye, Abs."

"'Bye."

I disconnect the call and drag myself to my closet. Sliding open the door, I glance at my meager selection of clothing options. I really need to unpack my shit but doing so would mean I'm staying in Boston and my life in Hoboken, everything Steve and I built over the past five years, is really over. Massive sigh.

I flip through some hangers, wondering what to wear. Mary and Joe Merrick were my parents closest friends when we lived in Boston. Drew and their eldest daughter, Savannah, were in the same grade as school just like me and their son Austin. As kids, Austin and his sisters, Savannah and Claire, were more like mine and Drew's cousins. We pretty much grew up around their kitchen island and in their backyard. Summer nights catching fireflies with Claire and her cousin Indy, winter mornings sledding with Austin and Drew, and a very memorable shopping experience with Savannah, round out some of my favorite childhood memories.

Austin Merrick was once my closest friend but always in the-boy-next-door kind of way. If something was truly wrong, I could count on him for advice. But in our daily interactions, he was often more annoying than Drew. He made fun of me the first time I shaved my legs, cut the colorful, glitter tassels off the handlebars of my bike, and hid my rock collection for an entire weekend.

As we grew older and Austin became a hockey star, we

drifted apart. In high school, he ran with the cool kid crowd while I was more of the bookish, geeky set. Even though he was crazy popular, with girls flocking to hang off his shoulders or get a ride home in his souped up Infiniti G35, I still looked at him and saw the boy who pantsed me at a family vacation in Martha's Vineyard.

Despite the vast difference in our social stratas, Austin *was* always nice to me at school. It was me who added the final distance to our friendship. Halfway through our freshman year, I stopped getting rides home from him because it drew too much ire from his fan club. After that, I rarely saw Austin close-up unless it was a family gathering and he often missed those due to hockey. By the time my family relocated to New York at the end of my sophomore year, Austin and I were acquaintances at best. Afterwards, we lost touch completely, and my only updates about his life came via my mom or Savannah when our paths crossed in New York.

Now, he's the captain of the NHL Boston Hawks, something my dad shares with every single hockey fan he encounters. My parents pride for Austin knows no bounds.

Will he be at dinner tonight?

Probably not. He must be way too busy with his career, his team just won the Stanley Cup for crying out loud, to have dinner with me and my parents.

I finger a simple, summer dress.

Does it matter if he's there?

For a blink, Austin's piercing blue eyes, the color of the Atlantic in October, when winter's creeping in, flare in my mind. Even as the girl-next-door, I can objectively admit that he was always devilishly handsome, with quick eyes, and a sly smirk. He was a notorious rule breaker although he was too charismatic to ever face discipline for the trouble he stirred up. He was popular, likable, and infuriatingly immature. Way back when, he used to wear spicy cologne and oversized hoodies. He asked me to dance at the Valentine's

Day dance my freshman year after my date kissed another girl.

I pull the summer dress off the hanger. Where did that thought even come from? This isn't some trip down memory lane. I'm tagging along with my parents while they visit their friends. I'm not rekindling a friendship with Austin, a guy who is now larger than life. I probably don't even register on his radar, save for a handful of childhood memories.

Man, Steve did a number on my head if I'm even thinking about Austin at all.

I shimmy into the summer dress. I slip into simple, strappy sandals and find a pair of earrings in my purse.

Austin's not going to be at dinner tonight. Neither is Savannah, since she lives in New York City. We'd occasionally meet for lunch before my life turned upside down and I was too embarrassed to see friends, save for Abbi.

If anything, I should hope Claire or Indy make an appearance so I can reconnect with girlfriends. At least they may invite me out with them.

My phone buzzes with an incoming message and I swipe it up, assuming it's Abbi.

Mimi: I hope your heart's not too broken to notice Austin Merrick.

I snort. I swear, Mimi is more of a troublemaker than Austin. At eighty-four, she's sharper than a whip and more meddlesome than Mom.

Me: I doubt he'll even be there.

Mimi: He's a good boy. Sees his Mom and Dad once a week for dinner. He'll be there.

Eye roll.

Me: Even if he is, he won't remember me.

My phone rings.

"Mimi, I regret ever teaching you to text," I answer.

She chuckles, her warm laughter spreading through the line and right through me. As much as the reason *why* I'm back in Boston pains me, spending time with Mimi is a definite plus. "I would have learned without you."

"I don't doubt it."

"Why don't you think Austin will remember you? You used to *bathe* together for crying out loud."

I wince at the visual because imagining a man like Austin *bathing* now...well, I shouldn't imagine that while on the phone with my octogenarian grandmother.

"I haven't seen him in a decade." I point out.

"He was at your parent's Christmas party a few years ago."

I squint, as if that will somehow help me recall the evening in question. It comes back slowly, the clink of glasses, the sparkle of tinsel on the tree, and I vaguely recall seeing the Merrick family, Austin included. But that Christmas, I only had eyes for Steve. I barely remember anything other than my intense feelings for him.

"Hmph. He'll more than remember you, Chloe Ann. What I don't like is you needing me to remind you of this. Steve deserves a good talking to after the way he treated you. In my day —"

"Mimi."

She sighs. "I know, I know. It's none of my concern how you squander your twenties."

I wince at her honesty, feeling very much like I wasted the second half of the decade wrapped up in Steve's life instead of cultivating my own.

"What are you wearing to dinner?" Mimi changes the subject.

I describe my sundress and she makes noncommittal sounds that make me laugh. "Get any ideas of playing matchmaker right out of your mind," I say. "If Austin is there, he'll be polite and charming, the way he always is."

"I'll say. That boy could charm the pants off of —"

"Goodnight, Mimi."

"Bring me doughnuts tomorrow morning. I want to know how big his biceps are now. And how he's handling all the pressure now that he's *won* the Stanley Cup. Won it, Chloe! He always did carry the weight of the world on his shoulders."

I roll my eyes because that's a stretch if I've ever heard one. But Mimi has always had a soft spot for the reckless athlete.

She's still muttering when I gently remind her that I need to get ready.

"Oh, yes. Don't forget about your eyebrows. If you pencil them in neatly, you won't have to do that micro blading that's all the rage these days. Although, in my day we did tattooing too you know. I can still teach you —"

"Mimi."

"Love you, Chloe girl. Have fun tonight. Real fun. With Aus—"

I disconnect the call, muttering to myself. Even though Mimi has an uncanny ability to predict my life, she's wrong about this one.

I haven't thought about Austin Merrick since high school. Dinner at his parent's house isn't going to change that.

I eat my words.

I eat them all so quickly I choke on them.

Because when the door to the Merrick home swings open, I'm greeted by the same intense blue eyes of my teenage years. My mouth drops open and the irrational thought of how the hell I ever forgot about Austin zips through my mind.

How does anyone forget a man who looks like, well, *him*?

"Chloe Crawford," Austin murmurs, giving me a sly smirk before greeting my parents.

I can hardly process the fact that he's here, looking like a sex god mated with a Roman one, as Mary and Joe pull me into their embraces and welcome me back to Boston. A whirlwind of exclaimed greetings and hugs unfolds in the foyer.

"You didn't have to bring anything," Mary says, her eyes shining as she kisses Mom hello and thanks Dad for the two decorative wine sleeves he hands her.

"We're so happy you're back," Joe chimes in, wrapping an arm around my shoulders.

I grin up at him, remembering the pep talks he used to give Savannah, Claire, and me when the neighborhood boys would exclude us from their hockey and basketball games.

Mary leads the adults into the kitchen but I hang back, my gaze finding Austin's. He's leaning against the closet door, his hands stuffed into the pockets of his jeans, a thoughtful expression on his face.

"You look different," I blurt out, feeling my cheeks blaze.

He snickers. "It's been a minute."

"I didn't think you'd be here."

He winks. "But you're happy to see me, right?"

I roll my eyes and he grins. He's taller than I imagined and I have to crane my neck to look into his face. His smirk isn't as sly as it once was but his eyes are sharper, bolder, scanning mine with an intensity I feel down to my toes.

Strong shoulders, a broad chest, a tapered waist. *Stop checking him out!* I drag my eyes back to Austin's face, not missing the knowing glint in his eyes.

"It's good to see you again, Chlo." He straightens and holds his arms out for a hug like we're old friends. I guess, technically, we are.

But this feels different. Awareness unfurls throughout my limbs, my heart rate ticks up, and my skin tingles under

Austin's gaze. I feel like a hesitant teenager again, like my skin is too tight for all of the emotions trying to break free.

I step into Austin's embrace, my eyes closing of their own accord when he holds me close. His cologne wraps around me the way it always did but now, even that's different. His chest is hard and warm under my ear, just like I remember. But the arms holding me now are the arms of a man and I want to sink into their strength more than I should.

A hell of a lot more than a woman with a broken heart and an uncertain future should think about.

Read *The Rule Maker* now!

HEY READER

Hi lovely reader!

Thank you so much for reading *The Faker!* I'd love to know your thoughts on Torsten and Rielle. It would mean so much to me if you would please leave a *review*. If you're loving Boston Hawks Hockey, don't miss out on Austin Merrick's book, *The Rule Maker*, now available.

If you're interested in learning more about my books, please sign up for my monthly newsletter. It's full of updates, sales, free reads, and a new romantic, military suspense serial, *Protecting Amie*. Or, come hang out in my Facebook Reader Group, Gina Azzi's Book Besties.

Thank you so much for all of your support.

XO,
  Gina

ALSO BY GINA AZZI

Knoxville Coyotes Football:

Faked and Fumbled

Surprised and Sacked

Trapped and Tackled

The Burnt Clovers Trilogy:

Rebellious Rockstar

Resentful Rockstar

Restless Rockstar

Tennessee Thunderbolts:

Hot Shot's Mistake

Brawler's Weakness

Rookie's Regret

Playboy's Reward

Hero's Risk

Bad Boy's Downfall

Lock 'Em Down

Boston Hawks Hockey:

The Sweet Talker

The Risk Taker

The Faker

The Rule Maker

The Defender

The Heart Chaser

The Trailblazer

The Hustler

The Score Keeper

Second Chance Chicago Series:

Broken Lies

Twisted Truths

Saving My Soul

Healing My Heart

The Kane Brothers Series:

Rescuing Broken (Jax's Story)

Recovering Beauty (Carter's Story)

Reclaiming Brave (Denver's Story)

My Christmas Wish

(A Kane Family Christmas

+ *One Last Chance* FREE prequel)

Finding Love in Scotland Series:

My Christmas Wish

(A Kane Family Christmas

+ *One Last Chance* FREE prequel)

One Last Chance (Daisy and Finn)

This Time Around (Aaron and Everly)

One Great Love

The College Pact Series:

The Last First Game (Lila's Story)

Kiss Me Goodnight in Rome (Mia's Story)

All the While (Maura's Story)

Me + You (Emma's Story)

Standalone

Corner of Ocean and Bay

ACKNOWLEDGMENTS

Rielle Carter and Torsten Hansen have been clamoring around in my mind for months. I spent so much time envisioning their romance that when it came time to write it, I could hardly stop! I wrote *The Faker* in three weeks and loved every second of it.

Of course, the finished product wouldn't be complete without some super special women. All of my thanks and gratitude to Becca Mysoor, Erica Russikoff, Amy Vox Libris, and Virginia Carey for their support, advice, insight, and attention to detail!

A million thank you's to Kate Farlow, Y'all. That Graphic. for designing an entire series of covers that I adore.

To MPP for keeping everything going. I love working with you and I'm so grateful for all of your support.

Many thanks to the fabulous ladies at Give Me Books Promotions! Thank you for helping me launch Rielle and Torsten's story into the world.

To all the incredible bloggers, reviewers, and readers, THANK YOU from the bottom of my heart for making my dream a reality! I hope you adore this book.

And to my family. T, A, R, L - love you to the moon and back.

ABOUT THE AUTHOR

Gina Azzi writes Contemporary Romance with relatable, genuine characters experiencing real life, love, friendships, and obstacles. She is the author of *Boston Hawks Hockey series, Second Chance Chicago series, Finding Love in Scotland series, The Kane Brothers series, The College Pact series, and Corner of Ocean and Bay.*

A Jersey girl at heart, Gina has spent her twenties traveling the world, living and working abroad, before settling down in Ontario, Canada with her husband and three children. She's a voracious reader, daydreamer, and coffee enthusiast who loves meeting new people. Say hey to her on social media or through www.ginaazzi.com.